W9-AGJ-003

w9/88

"You know what I'd like to happen now?"

Jago ran a finger across the back of Erin's wrist. "I'd like us to wander upstairs and make slow, easy love."

"Jago!" Erin's brown eyes were troubled.

"I wouldn't start exclaiming in that horrified tone of yours," he murmured. "I'm not asking you for a one night stand.... Trust me."

"I can't." Erin swallowed. "It's not that I don't like you because I do, but—"

"I'm not talking about *liking* dammit!" He glowered at her, snatching his fingers from hers. "Our coming together is against your professional ethics, that's why you're getting so uptight again. Tell me, are we allowed to fraternize once the book's published? There has to be more to life than putting words on paper." Jago caught hold of her hand again. "Doesn't there?"

ELIZABETH OLDFIELD began writing professionally as a teenager after taking a mail order writing course, of all things. She later married a mining engineer, gave birth to a daughter and a son and happily put her writing career on hold. Her husband's work took them to Singapore for five years, where Elizabeth found romance novels and became hooked on the genre. Now she's a full-time writer in Scotland and has the best of both worlds—a rich family life and a career that fits the needs of her husband and children.

Books by Elizabeth Oldfield

Don't miss any of our special offers. Write to us at the following address for information on our newest releases.

Harlequin Reader Service
901 Fuhrmann Blvd., P.O. Box 1397, Buffalo, NY 14240
Canadian address: P.O. Box 603,
Fort Erie, Ont. L2A 5X3

ELIZABETH OLDFIELD

bachelor in paradise

Harlequin Books

TORONTO • NEW YORK • LONDON
AMSTERDAM • PARIS • SYDNEY • HAMBURG
STOCKHOLM • ATHENS • TOKYO • MILAN

Harlequin Presents first edition March 1987
ISBN 0-373-10964-4

Original hardcover edition published in 1986
by Mills & Boon Limited

CHAPTER ONE

HE looked *ordinary*.

Yet another fantasy bites the dust, Erin thought, a wry smile inching its way across her mouth. From the start she had treated Cleo's superlatives with healthy disdain, and now she was being proved right. As with so many of his breed, the man's appeal could be attributed ten per cent to being photogenic and ninety per cent to publicity hype. The smile edged dangerously close to a giggle. This was Super Stud? Oh dear, her agent would have been disappointed.

Shading her eyes against the dazzle which came off the pool, she walked closer. The man asleep on the candy-striped lounger was muscled and tanned to be sure, yet no more muscled or tanned than any of the young men she had seen that morning during her jog. Florida must be packed with such males, and most would be a darn sight more presentable than this one.

Golden stubble glinted on his jaw. He was badly in need of a shave. Not that a shave would transform him into anything spectacular. His chin would continue to be too angular, the line of his nose too sharp and most decidedly skew-whiff. At least he was a natural blond, which was something to be said in his favour, but what had happened to that flowing tawny mane, the Jago Miles trademark? In his role of TV heart-throb he wore his hair overlong, parted in the middle. Two vital wings sprang down

across his brow; wings destined to be brushed aside
with piratical verve or run through by feminine
fingers at what seemed to be monotonous three-
minute intervals. But this morning's sleeping
position and the heat had combined to flatten his
hair damply to his head. So much for leonine
splendour!

Curiosity drew Erin round the corner of the pool.
From the slump of his long body, the creases in his
sawn-off shorts, it was obvious he had spent the
entire night there. Why? She cast a glance over her
shoulder. If the white Hollywood-style villa, with its
green tiled roof and sweeping porches, was half as
grand inside as out, there would be a king-size bed
in a king-size room waiting for His Majesty. Had an
excess of alcohol caused his collapse? Maybe high
jinks with a girl, or several girls, had rendered him
too drained to crawl up from the poolside?
Recalling the magazines she had scanned, anything
seemed possible. Jago Miles was not the type to
settle for cocoa, a good book and an early night.

Suddenly she stopped. Her sense of purpose had
begun to wobble. Waking him would be presumptuous. In any case, nine o'clock on a Sunday morning
was a little early to come calling. She had never
intended to call, but the time difference had had her
rising from her motel bed at an indecently early
hour. Itchy with an urge for action, Erin had
decided to explore. According to her guide book,
the island was an 'exotic semi-tropical wonderland
of silver beaches and tranquil lagoons, studded with
some of the most luxurious real estate on Florida's
west coast', and so she had set off. Clad in Sloppy
Joe T-shirt and short shorts, with a cotton hat as
protection against the already strong sunshine, Erin

had jogged along the beach, cut up through parkland and skirted the approach to the narrow causeway which connected the island to the mainland. Whilst on the move it had seemed sensible to check that the actor's home was situated where the motel receptionist had said it would be and, approaching along a palm-tree-lined lane, she had discovered the wrought iron gates wide open. Open gates had appeared to symbolise a welcome, but . . .

Erin whipped off her sunhat and ruffled her long dark curls. Retreating to telephone later was more civilised. She would return to the motel three miles away, shower and change, then call to fix a formal appointment. Sunday presented a golden opportunity to introduce herself and set things in motion, because if contact was not made today when would Jago Miles next be available? Involved in churning out episode after episode of the soap opera *Taro Beach*, his workload would leave little breathing space. But suppose he had taken wing by the time she phoned? As one of the show business brigade wouldn't he possess an insatiable lust for getting out and about, making contacts, being seen?

With a sigh, Erin fixed the sunhat back on her head. Why had she ever allowed herself to be pushed into featuring him? It was *her* book, after all. Originally she had chosen to profile a portrait painter, a dentist, a mountaineer and a casino boss—then her agent and publishers had brought pressure to bear. She had been advised that if one of the quartet were American the book could be brought out in the States, and if that American happened to be well known, the venture would be more profitable all round. Economics mattered.

Accordingly Erin had drawn up a tentative list of senators, business tycoons, even an astronaut, but agent and publishers had combined to promote a different idea.

'We need someone with sizzle,' Cleo had explained. 'Think back and ask yourself who was responsible for nudging your book on women into the best seller list.'

'Patrice Lanham,' she had replied gloomily, then retaliated, 'but the other three women were far more . . . substantial.'

'I agree, yet it's a fact of life that an instantly recognisable household name attracts attention. Now, suppose we substitute the casino boss with Jago Miles? He's well known on both sides of the Atlantic, and as one of television's ten most eligible men has a tremendous following. I've already taken the precaution of having a word with his agent, and he says——'

'No thanks.' Erin's mouth had thinned. 'No way am I writing about a performing peacock again.'

'But he'd be perfect, and it's unreasonable to condemn an entire profession on the strength of one unfortunate incident. I know how you suffered at the hands of Patrice and co.,' Cleo had given her a sympathetic smile, 'but don't let that make you cynical. Thare's no reason to suppose Patrice and Jago Miles are two of a kind. If you include him in the book I guarantee your bank manager will smile for the next ten years. And don't tell me money's not important.'?

'I get by,' she had protested.

'Get by! Why eat mince when you're being given the chance to dine off fillet steak? Be smart.'

*　　*　　*

Erin scowled at the slumbering man. Cleo would award *him* top marks for being smart. Once a serious actor of promise, drawing critical acclaim for a controversial Hamlet, rave reviews for characterisations in Ibsen and Chekhov, two and a half years ago he had abruptly switched to playing the romantic lead in a soap opera. Thinking of the isolated episode of *Taro Beach* she had seen, she shuddered. How could he do it? *Taro Beach* wasn't even one of the better soaps. The answer was that it paid. For flicking back his hair and smiling a crinkle-eyed smile, he collected dollars by the truck load.

Erin sighed. The prospect of writing about a stereotype matinée idol was making her feel quite numb. All Jago Miles was likely to produce would be kiss-and-tell exposés, anecdotes geared to reveal, accidentally on purpose, what a devastating dream-boat he was. Gossip columns were the place for that kind of drivel. Patrice Lanham, whatever her personal shortcomings, had been a member of the English theatrical fraternity for more than forty years, and was dedicated to her art. This man wasn't dedicated. He didn't care.

Intent on departure, she turned, but a beer can, a full one, had been left standing at the rim of the pool and as she moved Erin knocked it with her foot. The can toppled over, rolled and fell into the water with a noisy plop.

'Oh!' she gasped, fingers flying to her lips.

The man on the lounger sat bolt upright. 'Susie? It's Susie?' he muttered, his tone fraught and strained.

'No. I'm——'

'You've come about Susie?' He blinked, struggling to awake. 'You're from——'

'The Driftwood Motel,' she supplied, when he broke off to grind two large fists into his eyes. Her bright smile was intended to be an apology for waking him. 'From England, really. I flew in last night.'

He staggered to his feet. He was taller than she had imagined, around six foot three. A hand was placed on the top of his head, as though it was whirling and needed to be steadied. The previous night must have been a hard one.

'You haven't brought news of Susie?'

Erin's smile became appropriately regretful. ' 'Fraid not.'

Ice-blue eyes, clear and deep-set, fixed on her. 'Then who the hell are you?' he demanded.

Jago Miles was not ordinary any more.

CHAPTER TWO

'MY name's Erin Page.'

'I take it I'm expected to leap up and down and shout "Wowee"?' he replied, unnerving her with a fast-freeze stare.

'Not—not really.'

He hooked his thumbs into his belt and yanked the denim shorts higher on to his hips. 'I don't know any Erin Page,' he said flatly.

'Yes, you do. Well, no, you don't.' He might be bedraggled, wearing only crumpled shorts, but of his presence there was no doubt. He emanated an energy which was impossible to ignore. His Hamlet must have been spine-tingling. 'But you remember my name? You must. Mr Steen said how much you were looking forward to meeting me.'

'Did he? Then I guess Mr Steen got carried away. It happens frequently.' His lip curled in a spasm of contempt. 'So you're one of Burt's bimbos? Hell, I thought at last I'd got it through to him that when I require feminine company I make my own arrangements. Sorry, but I'm not in the market for whatever it is you have to offer, and especially not at——' He squinted at the watch strapped to his wrist. '— nine-o-five in the morning. What do you think I am, some kind of push-button hormonal wizard?'

'You've got it wrong, Mr——'

'No, *you've* got it wrong,' he slammed. 'So kindly report back with the message "Thanks but no thanks." You might also add you're a shade too pale for my taste.' A sardonic brow lifted. 'Plus you're on the old side.'

'Old!' Indignation flushed away any nervousness. His attitude was offensive. She had not travelled all this way to be insulted by a lank-haired American, even if his middle name was supposed to be Mr Wonderful. Added to which she knew for a fact Jago Miles had been placed on this earth thirty-six years ago, half a dozen earlier than she had. She was too old? He was almost a museum piece! 'Maybe I'm not a nymphet with a suntan the colour of a leather saddle,' Erin retorted, 'but I can assure you that in some circles I'm——'

'In my circle——' He took a menacing step towards her. '— you are surplus to requirements.'

She stood firm, which required an effort with him bearing down like a barefoot gangster.

'I'm afraid you don't understand,' she said, relieved when he stopped a yard away. He was a big man. If he had picked her up bodily and thrown her in to join the beer can on the bottom of the pool she would not have been surprised.

'Damn right,' he barked, 'so why don't you explain? For a start I'd like a full account of how you managed to gain access to this property.'

'I came in through the front gates and—and I'm not here at Mr Steen's request.' Erin swallowed, unwilling to dwell on what it was the actor had imagined she had come to offer. 'Well, that's not quite true. Mr Steen did arrange——'

'Through the gates or over them? Or maybe you crept up from the beach?'

'I came *through* the gates.'

Jago Miles folded muscled arms across his chest,

a chest which she had to agree came up to glamour-
boy requirements. Broad and firm, it was covered
with the requisite mat of golden hair. And from his
chest a neat vertical line of body hair ran mid-centre
down the flatness of his belly to disappear into the
denim shorts.

'You bribed Rafael? I guess that wouldn't have
been too difficult.'

'I bribed no one. Least of all because no one was
there to bribe,' Erin said, growing impatient. 'The
gates were open and I walked up the drive. I
wondered about ringing the front door bell, but then
I caught sight of you here by the pool so I——' Her
hand sketched an investigative gesture. 'I dare say I
could be accused of trespassing, but——'

'You *are* trespassing,' came the swift
condemnation.

'But I wanted to see you.'

He rubbed his jaw, scowling when the stubble
rasped against his fingers. 'You mean you're a fan?'

'Good grief, no!' She broke out laughing. Did he
expect her to produce an autograph book? Beg for a
signed photograph? 'Er—yes,' she amended, her
thoughts skidding around like balls on a pin-table.
Jago Miles was an actor and as such would possess
an outsize ego. Admitting she was not an admirer in
such a definite way could be suicide. She must not
rile him, she must calm him. The aggression she had
unwittingly sparked off was counter-productive.
How could she write an account of his life without
his co-operation? Personal preferences must be set
aside, for her book's sake she must attempt to win
his acceptance and trust. 'I watch *Taro Beach* every
week,' she gushed.

'Then what's your opinion of my car, the silver

Maserati?' he questioned, the big freeze glare narrowing until his eyes resembled piercing blue icicles. Privately Erin christened him the Ice Man.

'It's—it's marvellous.'

'Don't lie. I thought you reckoned to have just come over from England, but the series lags a year behind there. The Maserati has yet to make an entrance.'

'I must be confused,' she blustered. 'Look, Mr Miles——'

'Yes, you must. It's my guess you're also confused about the gates being open. You're not a fan. Maybe I did wake up only a moment ago, but I'm not that dopey I can't recognise a sneak thief when I see one. The papers said there'd been a spate of daylight robberies.' He reached out to fasten a grip like a steel claw around har upper arm, and before she knew what was happening Erin found herself being roughly bundled along the side of the pool. 'What were you hoping to pick up—cameras, jewellery, a wallet stuffed with hundred-dollar bills? Save it for the cops,' he said, when she started to protest. 'I'm going to call them right now. A patrol car'll be round to collect you in minutes. With my troubles, you I really need,' he muttered, propelling her towards the house at breakneck speed. 'A sneak thief with big brown eyes, long legs and a sassy backside! It's true what they say, the bad guys look suspiciously like the good guys these days.'

'I'm not a thief,' she jabbered, half tripping in her attempt to pull free. 'I'm a writer.'

'Yeah?'

'*Yes.*'

The icicle look stabbed sideways. After a moment indecision glimmered across his face, and then he sighed. He appeared to believe her. This was an improvement, but only in the sense that the bow and arrow had been an improvement on the cudgel, for his expression continued to be stern, his fingers continued to bite into her arm, and his stride never faltered. Still she was being frog-marched towards the house.

'Not another goddamn journalist? I might have guessed.' Cold blue eyes scoured the smooth sweeps of grass and scarlet hibiscus bushes in the distance. 'Where's your pal with the camera? It's not like the paparazzi to miss a trick. Or has he already got what he wanted, courtesy of the long zoom lens?'

'You're mistaken,' Erin said, but was drowned out.

'Thief? Journalist? So what? You're still trespassing and I'm still calling the police.'

'Please do,' she hissed, furious at being hauled around like a common criminal. 'I don't care. I'm not a journalist, I'm a writer. There's a big difference. I write books, quality books, and you're due to be featured in one of them. It's been arranged for ages. My travel plans were finally agreed with Mr Steen a couple of weeks ago, and confirmed in writing.'

Jago Miles stopped dead. 'What the hell are you talking about?'

'You can't have forgotten.' Erin recognised he would lead a full life, but it couldn't be so full that combining with her on what was more or less a biography had slipped his mind—could it? A feeling of betrayal swamped her. Because the book absorbed her every waking moment she had automatically assumed the actor would regard his inclusion in it as—perhaps not earth-shattering, but

at least worthy of consideration. Not so. 'I'm
writing a factual account about four men from
different walks of life,' she explained. 'Last summer
discussions took place between Mr Steen and my
agent, Cleo Munro. It was agreed then you'd be one
of the quartet.'

The steel claw unfastened itself from her arm.
'This is news to me.'

'It can't be,' she protested.

'It is. I've seen no agreement, let alone put my
signature to one.'

'No, Mr Steen said it wasn't necessary, but——'

'And I have more publicity than I can handle
right now.'

'This isn't a PR thing,' Erin said earnestly. 'This
is an in-depth look at contemporary people and
their lives.'

'So?'

'So it's not just . . . candyfloss. Look, I've already
completed the profiles on the other three men, why
don't I let you read them and——'

'Pass.'

Must he be so damned arrogant? Must his refusal
sound so definite? In retrospect it was clear Cleo
should have insisted on some kind of formal
contract. But perhaps he was just playing hard to
get? Perhaps he wanted to be coaxed?

'Mr Miles,' she began, remembering how Patrice
Lanham had been a glutton for flattery, no matter
how thickly it was trowelled on.

'Miss Page,' he countered 'You are becoming a
nuisance.'

'Mr Miles, as a man of our times the public are
fascinated by your views, your opinions, your
lifestyle.' Erin spoke quickly, intent on preventing

an interruption. 'It's not everyone who was once called the thinking woman's Adonis, and——'

'The what? Jeez!' He threw back his head and laughed, only to sober in double-quick time. The chill look returned. 'Nice try, but the answer remains the same. I'm not in the mood to be dissected, even if it is by a quasi-sociologist, so I'd be grateful if you'd quit hassling me and go.' He jabbed a long index finger towards the front of the house. 'Go!'

Her heart sank, her insides felt nipped. Erin could recognise a genuine rejection when she heard one. But where did that leave her? The interviews with the mountaineer had taken longer than expected, due to his habit of disappearing without notice to scale remote crags, and now the deadline for completion of her manuscript was fast approaching. Two months in Florida to assemble information and draft the profile, one month back home to finalise, her schedule was trimmed tight. And if she didn't write about Jago Miles, whom did she write about? Locating a suitable replacement at such short notice would be wellnigh impossible.

'But I've done the groundwork,' she told him, her voice straining upwards in distress.

'Go!' The ice developed a crack. 'If there's been some kind of mix-up, I'm sorry.'

'Are you? Well, it's a darn sight more than a mix-up,' Erin bit out. Why hadn't she followed her own wishes and insisted on interviewing the casino boss, come what may? Show business people were all suspect. Once before she had been the victim of the pick you up, drop you down technique, and here was Jago Miles, another supreme exponent of the art. His denial of all knowledge did not fool her. The notion of appearing in her book must have appealed last summer and down through each and every month until as recently as a fortnight ago, but on a whim he had changed his mind. Not in the mood— how dare he! 'You and your agent are nothing but a pair of con men,' she announced, yellow flecks glittering in the depths of her eyes. 'What am I expected to do? Put wasting my time and the cost of the air fare down to experience? Strange as it may seem, I don't appreciate experiences like that.'

'Suppose I go some way to reimbursing you?' Jago Miles suggested, striding across the patio. He opened sliding glass doors and directed her into a living-room where morning sunshine gilded plush white carpets, overstuffed leather couches in ice-cream colours, expensive furnishings. 'How much are you out of pocket—seven, eight hundred dollars?'

Erin glared. 'You imagine paying me off makes everything all right?'

'Can you suggest an alternative? Don't answer that,' he snapped, when she started to speak. 'I haven't time to stand and argue. There's someone I must visit this morning. It's important.' He went to a writing desk. 'A cheque will have to do. I don't keep that much cash in the house.'

'To hell with your cheque,' Erin blasted. 'I'm fully aware that standing in front of a camera like a reciting robot and indulging in gratuitous chest-baring has made you a wealthy man, but I wouldn't take a single penny. Maybe on the eighth day God was supposed to have created Jago Miles, but as far as I'm concerned he needn't have bothered because you are one of the most ill-mannered men I have ever met.' Her tongue was being reckless, but she did not care. She felt too strongly about the injustice of her situation—a situation *he* had dropped her into. 'Your initial salvo was that I'm in my dotage, next you accuse me of being a cat burglar, then you—you——'

Erin's tirade petered out. Her antagonist's attention had strayed. Head tilted, blond brows dipped in query, he was listening to the crunch of tyres on the drive. A car had arrived at the front porch.

'I wonder if this is Poll?' he muttered, and paced off through an archway to investigate.

Left alone, Erin stood and fumed. The man was not only a louse and an ignoramus, he was also committing sacrilege. What gave him the right to refuse to be featured in her book? Her other three subjects had been delighted—even honoured—to take part, acknowledging the seriousness of her work. They had had their priorities right, but not Jago Miles. Here she was, giving him the opportunity to gather kudos from appearing in an up-market dissertation, and all he could think about was girls. Poll. Susie. Less than ten minutes in his company and his fondness for females was in high profile. Erin wrinkled her nose in disgust. Didn't he know there was more to life than sex? Much more. Through the arch he was opening the front door and she waited, expecting the arrival of a juvenile and golden-skinned sex kitten. Instead a short, dark, thickset man in his early forties erupted into the house. He wore a vibrantly floral shirt and even more vibrantly checked trousers.

'Hi there, Jagie-baby,' he carolled, eyes twinkling behind gold framed spectacles. 'You're not going to like this but, please, before you say a word, hear me out. And trust me. There's this old broad arriving from England. My information is she's a top drawer writer. She wants to include you in——' Bounding through the archway, he saw Erin. 'Didn't realise you were entertaining,' he grinned. 'I'm sure sorry if I've burst in on a beautiful experience.'

'You haven't.' Jago's reply was verbal frostbite. 'And I suspect the old broad has arrived. Allow me to introduce Erin Page.'

'You're Erin? Here already?' After a split second of surprise, the newcomer bounced back. 'Gee, forgive me. I had this dumb image of an ancient bluestocking, but instead you're young and lovely.' He grabbed hold of her hand and pumped it up and down. 'Burt Steen. Great to know you.'

Faced with such an enthusiastic welcome, it would have been ungracious not to respond. 'How do you do,' she said stiffly.

'Get a load of that accent!' the agent exclaimed. 'Isn't it peachy?'

'Peachy.' Jago sniffed. 'Okay Burt, talk and talk fast. I don't know what stunt you're attempting to pull this time, but presenting me with Miss Page as a *fait accompli* won't work. I'm not prepared to be written up in some goddamn book. Since when did I need that kind of ego trip?'

'But this isn't just any old book. This is to be a prestige production, twenty-four carat class. Erin isn't your usual hack, oh no. She's an academic. She has a degree in history from——' Burt paused to smile at her like a dog show judge, '— Oxford.'

'Is that my cue for wild applause?' Jago demanded, flinging her a scurrilous look. Erin flung one back. Grudgingly she was being forced to accept that the actor seemed innocent of any trickery, but did that make much difference? She had still been brought out to Florida on a wild-goose chase. Maybe Burt Steen was the real villain of the piece, but blaming client rather than agent felt far more satisfactory. 'If Miss Page translates Homer for kicks, sings madrigals and wears pince-nez, heigh jolly ho.' Jago had lapsed into a sneering English voice. 'But count me out.'

'Ease up. You're too tense. Your shoulders are knotted. Aren't his shoulder muscles knotted?' Burt appealed to Erin. He patted the actor's arm. 'I can tell you're short on sleep, buddy, and I sympathise. I know what you're going through. But trust me. The bottom line is that this book's going to be a best seller. Erin writes best sellers.'

'I've written one,' she felt compelled to point out. Burt's persuasive tactics might be in her own interests, but the truth remained important.

'This'll be another.' The agent spoke with the authority of someone who had his own private crystal ball. 'And when the book hits the top of the pile, Jagie-baby, you'll make bucks.'

'I benefit financially?' Her antagonist swung to her. 'You never said anything about that.'

'I didn't have much opportunity, did I?' she shot back, then added, 'The arrangement is that in return for your co-operation you'll receive a share of the royalties. Mr Steen has full details, has had them for over nine months.'

Burt's smile was blithe. Despite evidence to the contrary it was clear that in his own mind he had dissociated himself from any malpractice, and now his round features radiated the desire to please.

'The deal's well worth consideration,' he assured Jago. 'As Erin's here, why not give it a spin? This time next year you could be kicking yourself if you don't. Get my drift?'

'Yeah.' A look passed between the two men, and the blue eyes which travelled to Erin took on a speculative glint. 'You reckon there's a chance of this book doing well?'

'It's possible, though naturally I can't promise a surefire success. The public are unpredictable and much depends on what else is being brought out at the same time. However, my writing has achieved a certain level of respect.' Her tart tone indicated it was high time he showed her some. 'Cleo reckons the profiles I've already submitted are better than anything I've done before, so the book looks . . . hopeful.'

'How many books have you written?'

'Five. Four Edwardian biographies and the companion to this one, which featured the lives of contemporary women.'

'Didn't I tell you this chick has pedigree?' Burt chimed in.

'You look too young to have written five books,' Jago said suspiciously.

Erin dispensed a sweet smile. 'Ten minutes ago you were telling me I was too old.'

'Yes. Well.' The bramble on his chin was scratched. 'Burt, you and I need to talk. Drive Miss Page over to her motel, then come and fill me in.' He turned to Erin again. 'We'll get back to you on this.'

The Ice Man had dismissed her.

Lying on the bed, Erin stared at the ceiling. For two hours she had been anticipating Burt Steen's promised call, but there had been no contact. Now she was on the brink of lifting the telephone,

requesting Cleo's number and advising her agent to
expect her back on the first available plane. Why
should Jago Miles be allowed to play God? She
deeply resented being forced to hang around
waiting for him to deign to say an icy yea or nay,
and even more so when it was clear any yea would
stem entirely from financial considerations. It had
amazed her how his attitude had changed at the
mention of cash—amazed and sickened. If he had
stuck to his guns and refused to be written up come
hell or high water, Erin would have granted him
certain admiration, but instead he had reinforced
the image of himself as a person willing to do
anything for money. And much wanted more. Yet
in comparison with the well documented salary he
drew from *Taro Beach*, his share of the royalties
would be pocket-money. Pocket-money he would
doubtless drool over.

Lost in contemplating his greed, she was taken by
surprise when the telephone shrilled.

'Erin-baby, we have lift off,' announced a
triumphant Burt. 'Jago's ready and waiting, itching
to get started. I'll collect you from the motel in
fifteen minutes, okay?'

A hair's breadth away from saying, 'Nuts to Jago
Miles' and slamming down the receiver, Erin
remembered her deadline. Like it or not, she *needed*
the man.

'Okay,' she agreed.

A quarter of an hour later she was sitting beside
Burt in an electric blue Cadillac, listening as he did
his best to make amends.

'Once you get to know him, you'll realise Jago's a
real nice person. He might be a star, but his head

hasn't been turned. The guy genuinely believes he's nothing special.'

'Fancy that,' she remarked, but her sarcasm went unnoticed.

'What you gotta remember is that Jago's living under pressure. The *Taro Beach* schedule means he's up at dawn and doesn't get home until gone eight each evening. There'll be a break in ten weeks' time, but that's way off. At the moment it's go, go, go.' He flashed her a smile. 'Isn't it understandable if occasionally he gets uptight, blows his top? Yeah. Added to which you've met him at a very stressful period because——'

'Because what?' Erin prompted, when he clammed up.

The agent braked slightly as he swung the car onto the private lane, then continued smoothly, 'Because he's experiencing some aggression from Kiel.' Kiel, it transpired, was a 'good-looking dude with ebony hair' who played Jago's long-standing enemy in *Taro Beach*. 'Problem is, on screen the guy's as lively as cardboard and he knows it. In retaliation he works out his hostility on the rest of the cast, but mainly on Jago. It bugs him that Jago gets twice the fan mail. Though he would, wouldn't he—being a legend in his own lifetime?' Burt remarked, displaying the skills of a megalomaniac public relations man.

Erin's mouth twitched. ' "See, the conquering hero comes!" ' she recited. ' "Sound the trumpets, beat the drums!" '

'Gee, is that Shakespeare?' breathed her companion.

'Thomas Morell.'

Their arrival at the entrance to the villa fore-stalled any questions as to Morell's identity, and this time the gates were indeed closed. Burt was required to sound his horn once, twice, three times, before a sleepy Hispanic teenager stumbled from the bushes to be identified as the truant Rafael. Yawning, the boy dragged open the gates and stood aside as they cruised on to the drive.

'Jago said for you to go straight in,' Burt explained, depositing her beneath the porch. He climbed back into his car and gave a genial wave. 'Have a nice day.'

'I'll try,' she muttered.

Briefcase tucked beneath her arm, Erin walked through the open door and into the entrance hall. Assuming a greeting at any moment, she stood and waited. And waited. She brushed a shiny, freshly shampooed curl from her shoulder, adjusted the belt of her navy linen dress, and coughed politely to warn of her arrival. Nothing happened. Through the archway the living-room spread itself in unoccupied splendour. All she could hear was the distant whirr of an air-conditioner. She coughed again. She had not expected Jago Miles to lay on red-carpet treatment, but she had expected him to be here. Erin waited. Still nothing. Burt's insistence that the actor was itching to get started appeared to be baloney, like so much else.

'Mr Miles?' She peeped into a dining-room, then a sleek modern kitchen. There was no sign of life. 'Mr Miles?' She stood in the middle of the hall. '*Mr Miles!*'

'Come on up,' called a far-away voice.

Her fists clenched. She could have killed him. Not only did he lack the courtesy to meet her in the proper manner, now he expected her to go chasing up the stairs after him. Erin took a fierce step forward, then halted abruptly. Although he had seemed anything but enamoured, was it possible Jago Miles could be waiting for her in his bedroom, like a spider luring a fly? She viewed the staircase with wary eyes. She had no intention of walking into a trap. Hadn't she had trouble before with a man who, in the belief he was irresistible, had pounced when least expected? She was weighing up whether being too pale and too old could be interpreted as meaning she was immune from seduction, when a figure appeared on the landing. As he leant over the railing she saw that the lower half of his face was covered in creamy white foam.

'Hi. Come along up and then you can tell me what you want,' he ordered, and promptly vanished.

Erin stood and stared at the empty space. She felt dazed. What *she* wanted? Had the Ice Man melted to become Santa Claus? Intrigued, and deciding that someone smothered in shaving soap would scarcely be milliseconds away from ripping the clothes off her, she fixed her briefcase more securely under her arm and mounted the stairs. A faint rasping sound guided her to a bathroom. Through the open door she saw Jago Miles. He was standing before a mirror, cut-throat razor in hand, busy with the soaping, the scraping, the pained facial expressions necessary to remove stubble from jaw. The denim shorts had been exchanged for white drill slacks, but the tanned chest remained bare. The seal-like gloss of combed-back hair indicated he had recently stepped out of the shower.

'I suspect you'd have preferred me in jacket and tie, sat behind a desk,' he remarked laconically, in between slicing bubbles from his face in long, smooth strokes, 'but, like I told you, I had to go visiting. It's been one hell of a rush.' The evil cut-throat glinted. 'Give me a minute and I'll be with you.'

No, the Ice Man hadn't melted, though there had been a thaw of sorts, Erin decided, as she looked at him from the doorway. When previously encountered he had been strung up tight, now he seemed more relaxed. The prospect of extra dollars must have the same effect as tranquillisers, she thought acidly.

As she waited for him to finish, a strange yearning began to creep over her. How long had it been since a man had shaved in her presence? How many years since she had listened to a baritone sing off-key in the bath? Domestic intimacies came flooding back—the balled-up socks under the bed, a jacket tossed askew, masculine paraphernalia cluttering the bathroom shelf. Mesmerised, her eyes followed each movement as Jago cropped the final whiskers in a rasp of the razor which was almost sensuous. Remnants of soap were rinsed away, he checked his jaw, reached for a towel. The final touch was aftershave. Satisfied and unselfconsciously beaming at his reflection in the mirror, he slapped the liquid on his cheeks, wincing against the tingle. Lime-lemon spiced the air. Jago straightened, his task complete. Despite the angular jaw and skew-whiff nose, on him manhood looked good. Very good.

'Go ahead,' he said, as he reached for a fresh white shirt.

'My usual approach is to first have a series of general conversations. I need a fair amount on tape before I can decide which angle to pursue,' Erin explained, rattling off. She was grateful to be able to talk. Watching him, there had been a hurry in her blood which was both unexpected and unwelcome. 'Later, more specific topics can be discussed. I've listed your career from open-air theatre in Central Park to *Taro Beach*, but I've little on the other areas in your life. May I suggest we start with your childhood and take it from there?'

'My childhood?' He sounded surprised.

'Why not?'

'No reason, except that I've never been asked about my childhood before. Reporters restrict their questions to my adult life.' Jago gave her a quick glance as he buttoned his shirt. 'The emphasis being on my love life.'

'I'm not a reporter,' Erin pointed out firmly. 'And I'm interested in the man, not the myth.'

The crinkle-eyed smile made its first appearance. 'You reckon my love life's a myth?' He slid a large hand into the vee of his shirt where golden hair glistened, and massaged thoughtfully. 'As things stand at the moment, I guess you could be right. Okay, we'll start with my childhood.' He pursed his lips. 'You realise I don't have much free time? How about us sitting down together, say from nine until ten each evening, Monday through Saturday, will that do?'

'Is there any choice?'

'None.'

'Then it'll do.'

Jago tucked his shirt into his trousers, and walked with her along the landing. 'I'd better make it clear from the start that certain subjects are off-limits.'

'Like what?' she asked, immediately sensing trouble.

'I'll tell you when we come to them.' He saw her frown. 'Don't worry, we should be able to cobble together something decent.'

'Cobble something decent!' Erin stopped in her tracks. 'Mr Miles, it's obvious we're at cross-purposes here.'

'Call me Jago.'

'Jago,' she snapped. 'Well, Jago, if I'd wanted to cobble I'd have been a shoemaker. I'm not, I'm a writer. I write well-researched and factual accounts which have a beginning, a middle and an end. I have more respect for the reading public than to attempt to palm them off with something *cobbled* together.' The yellow flecks glittered in her eyes again. 'You may find this surprising, but my writing matters to me!'

'And my private life matters to me!' he shot back, then raised two placatory hands. 'Let's not fight, I think we've done enough of that for one day. As I see it, the position is this—I'm not ecstatic about being the subject of a profile, and I get the impression you're not over the moon at the prospect of writing about me. However, for various reasons we appear to be stuck with each other. I'm willing to play ball with you, if you're willing to play ball with me. Do we have a deal?'

Erin bit her lip. Not a word had been put on paper and already Jago Miles had announced his intention to call at least some of the shots. None of her other subjects, Patrice Lanham included, had thought it necessary to lay down rules beforehand.

They had trusted her. Why couldn't he trust her and simply co-operate? She was not a gutter press journalist, out for sensation. She had no wish to embarrass or cause distress. As someone who had incidents in her own life she would hate to have broadcast, she respected the privacy of the individual. That said, she was committed to writing the truth and, where possible, the whole truth. How could she interpret 'off-limits'? The term conjured up a bundle of images, all unwelcome. Was Jago Miles intending a wholesale deletion of incidents he felt might dent the Mr Wonderful image? Was his aim to trim away imperfections and nudge the facts into a more acceptable form? She could not agree to that. She had not come to Florida to script a superficial saga about a perfect person—nobody was perfect. Deep in thought, Erin walked down the stairs beside him.

'How far does this censorship of yours go?' she questioned.

'Not too far. Let me explain. One of the penalties of fame is that I'm considered to be public property and——' he grimaced, '— to a degree I accept that. What I don't accept is that the spotlight should also fall on my family. My parents are dead, but I have brothers and sisters, and protecting their privacy is important to me.'

His tone sounded eminently reasonable, and the problems Erin had visualised a moment ago receded. She gave a pert nod.

'It's a deal.'

'Good. Now, what else do you require apart from chat?'

'A glance at anything which mentions your name. Items from school, college, theatre programmes, whatever. The majority won't be used, but I'd be grateful to have the chance to select and reject.'

They had reached the living-room. Jago indicated a seat, and dropped down on the couch opposite. He reached for a packet of cigars. 'You're in luck. I have four tea chests stuffed full with papers.'

'Four!' Her biographer's spontaneous rush of delight at the prospect of such goodies was rapidly tempered. Jago Miles might be co-operating, but wasn't she being offered the collection of an egomaniac? Papers would doubtless mean reviews, though never bad ones; photographs, but never those taken from an unflattering angle; articles, buttered with calorific compliments. If he was like Patrice, he would be addicted to self-gratification. The actress's 'papers' had been arranged in a score of albums, each a visual hymn of praise of which she had never wearied. 'I'd like to take a look,' Erin said, trying her best to sound keen.

'Fine.' He pushed a hand through his hair, hair which as it dried was rapidly becoming a thick mane of burnished gold. 'Though here and now I disclaim any responsibility for you winding up cross-eyed. My mother wrote small, neither could she spell.'

'Your mother? I don't understand.'

'Ursula never threw anything away, so the tea chests contain a lifetime's collection of memorabilia, or trash—whichever you prefer. The rest of my family were all set to burn the lot after she died, but somehow I felt——' What Jago felt was left to her imagination. 'Amongst the papers are her diaries. I mention them because you said you were interested in my childhood and the diaries contain references to me. Not many though,' he warned.

'I'll read them.' Erin took a determined breath. 'And may I examine reviews, press cuttings etc?'

He lit the cigar. 'See Burt, he keeps track of such things. Anything else?'

'Oh, er——' Such a peremptory dismissal of the scrapbook syndrome left her stumbling. 'I'd like permission to speak to a few people about you.'

'Elaborate,' came the request.

'The one dimensional approach has a tendency to be flat, and I'd prefer to pep up the profile with a quote or two from different sources—say from Mr Steen and work colleagues. I'm not on the prowl for gossipy titbits,' she assured him when he looked hesitant. 'I just want snippets of additional information.'

'Okay, but check anything Burt might say with me.' The crinkle-eyed smile returned. 'You'll have gathered that he's an atrocious liar.'

'Will do,' Erin grinned, delighted to see how the Ice Man's thaw was continuing. 'Would it also be possible for me to visit the *Taro Beach* set and watch you at work?'

'Shouldn't be any problem. The entire team'll be here next Sunday for a barbecue, why not join us? You could have a word with William, our director, and set something up.'

'Thanks.' She took her tape recorder from her briefcase. 'Shall we make a start on your childhood right now?'

'You're quite a whirlwind of efficiency, aren't you?' he commented, looking amused.

'That's the way I work.' Erin pressed the appropriate switch. 'Fire ahead.'

'I was born in Thailand on the seventh of

October, nineteen hundred and——'

'Thailand?' she queried in surprise.

He nodded. 'My parents were on a Siamese kick at the time. My father was an architect, my mother a sculptress. They'd gone out there to look for inspiration. Such trips weren't unusual. My parents, my mother especially, had a definite bent towards the nomadic. As a result I attended more schools than I have fingers and toes.' He took a pull on his cigar. 'I was the first of six children born to John and Ursula Miles, or Ursula Liden, as my mother preferred to be known. She was one of the original feminists. When you read the diaries you'll realise she was very much an independent spirit.'

'Ursula Liden?' The name rang a bell and Erin tried hard to remember. 'Swedish-American,' she declared, after a moment. 'She did a tondo which created a tremendous controversy at the time. It was commissioned by a Viennese art foundation, but when the sculpture was delivered the trustees rose up in horror and demanded it be removed. Eventually the tondo was sited on a headland near—near——'

'Rio. But how do you know this? The tondo gained its notoriety more than twenty years ago. Added to which, Ursula's press coverage was a flash in the pan. She never produced anything else of note.'

'One of the men featured in my book is a painter. We were discussing the various forms of art one afternoon and he mentioned the tondo. He said it represented a powerful pagan image.'

'Others likened it to an extremely obscene rock cake,' Jago said with a laugh. 'But we're digressing.' He had another drag at his cigar. 'From day one I lived what I suppose you could only call a pretty bohemian existence.'

Erin leant forward. The numbness had gone, adrenalin was flowing. Contrary to being a 'what you saw, was what you got' Tinsel Town product, Jago Miles had hidden depths. And the paramount purpose in her life was to plumb them.

CHAPTER THREE

THE first few days were spent becoming acclimatised and establishing a routine. Erin arrived at the sprawling white villa each morning on the dot of nine, broke for lunch at one, then worked through until six. She returned to the motel for dinner, retracing her route mid-evening when she met up with Jago for their conversations.

'Use the back bedroom as your study,' he had suggested, and so she was installed, together with typewriter, tape recorder and the four tea chests.

'Back bedroom' seemed a tame description for the sumptuous pink and white boudoir which overlooked the blue sheen of the Gulf of Mexico. As she sat at the desk attempting to decipher Ursula Liden's scribbles, so her eyes were drawn to the huge water-bed with its white satin coverlet. How many fevered couplings had taken place there? she wondered. Sinking to gossip column level she may be, but she could not help thinking that way. Burt had delivered vast files of cuttings, and although Erin had only glanced through, it had been noticeable how most included pictures of Jago with a stunning blonde or brunette draped all over him. Publicity was doubtless at the back, front and sides of some of these romances, but they could not all be make-believe. As a younger man his name had been linked with several women, and though on reaching thirty he appeared to have steadied down, there were mentions of an actress called Olivia, a live-in lover. Yet Olivia was in the past. Since his arrival in Florida two and a half years ago no serious relationships had been reported. Erin was reluctant to take his word about his love life being a myth, yet he did live alone—and in great style.

In addition to the boudoir there were three more bedrooms, each with bath, while downstairs the spread included gymnasium, sauna, games room, and a den with the largest television and stereo unit she had ever seen. So much space for one man, so much equipment, so much attention too, she thought, as Maria the housekeeper bustled in with morning coffee and cookies. Maria, aided by two other women, kept the house pristine, while outside three gardeners, a pool boy and the dozy Rafael tended to multifarious needs.

'The girls and me have been thinking, hon,' Maria announced, setting down the tray. 'We reckon you should move into the bungalow. The place is just sitting there doing nothing, and two months in a motel will cost you plenty. Most of your time is spent here already, so what's the difference? Would it help any if I speak to Jago about it?' she offered, sensing Erin's hesitation.

'Thanks, but no. I'm happy at the Driftwood.'

'Now hon,' Maria cajoled. 'As well as saving dough you'd be spared all that to-ing and fro-ing each day.'

'The Driftwood suits me fine,' Erin insisted. 'Really.'

With a smiling shrug of resignation the housekeeper departed, and Erin carried her coffee over to the window. By looking left, beyond the garage block, she could see the trim white bungalow sitting in the sunshine. Fully furnished and cleaned on a regular basis, it had been built to accommodate staff, but Maria and her cohorts went home each night. Erin sipped thoughtfully. Free lodgings would be attractive for her budget was tight, but wasn't Jago doing enough? Blighted with a mercenary streak the man might be, yet when it came to providing a work base, countless coffees, daily lunch and the use of his pool, he had shown no hesitation. Erin took another mouthful, thinking a touch sceptically that keeping her sweet was in his own interests—financial interests. He wanted her co-operation as much as she wanted his. Well, a move into the bungalow would serve *her* financial interests. Would it be presumptuous to float the idea? Why not? The Jago Miles of today was no longer the frosty Ice Man of last Sunday.

After such an ill-omened start, everything had gone surprisingly well. Maybe not so surprisingly, for Erin had done her best to make it happen that way. An advocate of positive thinking, she had made a determined effort to gain his acceptance and now—it was Friday—felt that a pat on the back was warranted. She did not claim all the credit for the way Jago had relaxed over the week—it could be that his relationship with Kiel had eased—but she had made a definite contribution. She had done her best to put his greedy *raison d'être* to the back of her mind and treat him as a committed contributor to her book. By nature she was a good listener, always fascinated by other people's experiences, so her interest in what he had to say was genuine. Jago had responded to that. Erin had 'played ball', and he had more than done his share.

At the appointed hour of nine each evening, he had sprawled in a chair with a cheroot between his fingers, a tumbler of whisky close by, and reminisced in a low American drawl which was easy on the ears. That he could work such long hours and talk informatively and coherently at the end of the day was a source of constant wonder—and thanks. Erin had seen how tired he was, detected lines of strain, yet he never complained. For his discipline, he had gained her gratitude.

It had to be admitted that at first her encouraging smiles had been underscored with suspicion. As someone with a stated lack of enthusiasm for the project was he going to shortchange her, tell half-truths, fob her off with inaccurate flashbacks which had gathered a gloss through years of repetition on the party circuit? But his reminiscences were genuine and spontaneous. Erin had conducted sufficient two-way exchanges to be able to spot the trotted out phrase, a rehearsed recital, and although on the alert had found him guilty of neither.

Coffee cup empty, she returned to work. Her scrutiny of the diaries had only just begun. Blessed—or was it cursed?—with a methodical nature, she had first felt it necessary to remove every single piece of paper from the tea chests and arrange them in some kind of order. The chore had not been simple. On her knees for hours on end, Erin had filled the dust-sheet around the desk with mountainous piles of postcards, letters, sketches and travel documents which spanned fifty years. Each had been inspected, her biographer's curiosity had insisted on that, but now she accepted she had been wasting her time. If the thirty-thousand-word profile had featured Ursula Liden the items would have been of interest, but they contained few items of information pertinent to her son.

Would the diaries be equally deficient? Jago had warned of minimal references, and the diaries she had read so far had indicated that his mother was not the type to wax lyrical in print over a child. Still, if nothing else they would confirm Jago had been where he said, when he said. Erin turned a page, and then another.

'I'm sure my eyeballs have much in common with a road map of Central London,' she said that evening, as she changed tapes in her recorder. 'Your mother's writing is diabolical.'

'Highly individualistic, like her. But after causing problems all your life, why stop just because you're dead?' Jago grinned and lit a small brown cheroot. 'India,' he murmured, 'that comes next.'

'India?'

'See how fortunate you are, having me to bring a spot of colour into your otherwise drab existence?'

'But a moment ago you were in New York. Your second sister had just been born.'

'Ah, then Ursula was beset by the urge to inspect Hindu carvings.'

Erin sat back, her eyes wide. 'So the whole family upped and went with a new baby—just like that?'

'Don't sound so scandalised. People do do these things.' Jago looked at her from beneath thick blond brows. 'Though maybe not your kind of people.'

That was very true. Erin's growing up had taken place in a cosily confined environment. The sole offspring of doting parents, she had been born and bred in a quiet English village; the same village where she lived now. As a child she had known few surprises, and also few shocks. Jago's upbringing was one long shock. How she would have coped with the 'pretty bohemian existence' she dreaded to think. Yet he spoke easily, uncomplainingly about the endless upping of roots, the wandering minstrel travels, the non-conformist mother and often absent father. The baby in Thailand had taken its first steps in the States, toddled through Europe, started school in South America and at present the boy—Jago had reached his tenth year—was back in the States.

'No, it wasn't the whole family,' he corrected. 'My father was tied up with work, so he stayed behind.'

'Which means your mother gaily went off alone to India with what—four children?'

He nodded. 'My youngest brother and sister had yet to appear. Simmer down. You should know by now how unorthodox Ursula was.'

'Have you always called your mother Ursula?' Erin enquired, replacing 'unorthodox' with 'madcap'.

'From being able to talk, and my father was John. They wouldn't have it any other way. Said it broke down barriers.'

A gleam lit his blue eyes. 'Let me guess, you called your parents Mummy and Daddy, and still do?'

'Mum and Dad, actually.'

'Actually,' he mocked.

Erin refused to rise to the bait. Jago on a teasing kick had an alarming knack of quickening her blood, but she had not flown out to Florida in order for her red and white corpuscles to be exercised. She had flown out to write a profile, and maintaining a detached view of her subject was essential.

'Wasn't your mother frightened one of you might fall ill, or be allergic to the food? Wasn't she worried about the baby falling foul of the climate?'

'Ursula's mind didn't work that way. She was a creature of impulse. Her obsession was stone, nothing else came close. If someone told her about sculptures, a mountainside, even a quarry face which had some interest, off she went. Problems arising from day to day living never entered her head.'

'She chased around all over the world, dragging young children in her wake?'

Jago grinned. 'Wasn't it fortunate we all enjoyed travelling?'

'Was India . . . fun?'

'You wouldn't have enjoyed it.' His grin widened. 'We started off in a hotel, but Ursula miscalculated the currency, so after a week we swapped to the porter's uncle's house in downtown Bombay. The whole place stank of curry, and the bugs—jeez, the cockroaches were the size of porcupines. To compound matters Ursula's sense of time was shaky, so whenever she went off we could never be certain when she'd return. She was capable of getting carried away and watching patterns on stone from dusk, through moonlight, to dawn.'

Erin was aghast. 'Your mother left you on your own all night?'

'Occasionally, but the Indian family kept an eye on us, and don't forget I was a capable ten-year-old.'

'Ten's not much,' she retorted, remembering how her parents had insisted on babysitters until she was well into her teens.

'It was only me and the other two kids, she took the baby with her,' Jago explained, as though that corrected matters. 'Ursula was feeding my sister herself, so she travelled in a sling on her back.'

'Like a load of washing.' The words slid out of her mouth, the tone inferring *dirty* washing.

'Don't get prissy.' He squinted through a cloud of blue-grey smoke. 'I suppose any infant you had would sleep undisturbed in a padded crib?'

'In a silk-lined padded crib with frills, so there! And I'm not being prissy, I'm just wondering where routine and woolly winter vests and a lullaby at bedtime fit into all this.'

'They don't, but isn't it swings and roundabouts? My brothers, sisters and I may not have had the conventional mothering, but neither did we suffer the smothering. We were treated as adults and allowed to develop free from prejudices and pressures. Keeping up with the Joneses was unknown. Also we learned young that life isn't always smooth. When the bumps come we're immensely capable of clearing them.' Jago frowned, tapping the ash from his cigar. 'How many people can say the same?'

'I can,' Erin shot back, responding to the question as though it was a challenge.

'Yes?' He raised amused eyebrows. 'What do you know of life, real life? First it was Mum and Dad, then the ivory towers of Oxford, and now Burt tells me you live in a cute little cottage in a cute little village, with a cat.'

'What's wrong with having a cat?' she demanded, annoyed to discover Cleo must have discussed her with the brash Mr Steen.

'An unmarried girl with a pussy-cat who lives deep in the English countryside and for the most part spends her time scribbling Edwardian biographies?' He was laughing. 'My God! Miss Erin Page must have taken some knocks.'

'I'm not Miss Page. I'm Mrs Stuart. I'm a widow,' she informed him, indignant pink suns bursting on her cheeks. 'My husband died seven years ago. I write under my maiden name so it's simpler if I use the Miss. Peter's death was bumpy and——' Her mouth took on a bitter slant. 'And so was the period which followed. But I coped. It was what is called a "learning experience".'

Jago spread a hand. 'Then I apologise.'

'Apology accepted.'

'But you do live in a cottage?' he persisted. 'And you do have a cat?'

She nodded an irritated agreement. What had Cleo said? she wondered. Her agent often accused her of having become a backwater prude, acting like a dry as dust spinster, and this appeared to be the message which had buzzed across the Atlantic. Erin resented being viewed in that light. It was not true. Or was it? Her brown eyes clouded. Still, better to be thought of as a dry spinster and a prude than as a—as a what? Loose woman? Sexy little piece? How many times in the heat of passion had Ned called her his sexy little piece? Once the phrase had thrilled, made her feel wickedly alive and exciting. Now it infused her with shame. How could she have been so reckless, done such wild things?

'Have you lived alone since your husband's death?' Jago queried, and she jolted back to the present.

'I had a few months in London once, but let's get back to you in Bombay,' she replied swiftly. 'How did you deal with the cockroaches?'

'I wouldn't say we "dealt" with them, we just yelped when they scuttled across us in the night. It wasn't too bad,' he grinned, when Erin shuddered.

'On the whole we were adaptable kids.'

'Seems as though you had to be.'

'True. I remember once when——'

Back on the track, Jago talked about his Indian memories, and Erin gave herself a private lecture. Dwelling on her affair with Ned was degrading. It had been kept out of her head for ages and now she resolved it would stay out. Board that train of thought—Ned, lovemaking, her past abandonment, her present strait-laced control—and she was on a journey to nowhere.

'I'll call a cab,' Jago offered, when the proceedings came to a halt at ten o'clock.

The mention of transport brought to mind Maria's suggestion about the bungalow, and as he made the phone call she wondered how best to broach the subject. Back home the villagers would look askance on a young woman who suggested to a bachelor of known sexual prowess that she should live on his property, but where was the danger? Their relationship, though amiable, was a working one. The only thing they had in common was the profile.

'I seem to be becoming the taxi firm's best customer,' she remarked, when he said a cab was on its way. 'Three miles is too far to walk four times a day, so I'm back and forth, back and forth.' Her sigh slid down to her shoes. 'Pity I can't find a closer base.' Erin looked for a reply. 'Isn't it?' she prodded.

He yawned. 'What would you like, toots? A motel at the end of the drive? Try commuting between here and Miami each day like I do, then complain.'

'I'm not complaining.' She slipped her recorder into her briefcase. 'Maria tells me the bungalow's standing empty, all shiny and clean. Do you think it would be——'

'No, I don't. You can't,' Jago cut in, reading her mind. A heavy wing of tawny-blond hair was pushed from his brow. 'You can't move in because the bungalow's already let. Poll's taking up residence there next week.'

The poolside was crowded, and the patio, and the lawn. People sat round small tables, clustered in gossipy knots, weaved their way through the brightly dressed throng to return with plates piled high. Beneath the shade of a palm a white-hatted chef grilled steaks over glowing charcoal, while to one side guests chose from a vast array of salads. Waiters circulated, ensuring no one went without a drink, be it an exotic Caribbean cocktail or Perrier water. Conversation hummed. There was much laughter.

How different this gathering was from Patrice Lanham's claustrophobic 'at homes'. The actress had packed her London drawing-room full of supercilious snobs and bores, which meant Erin had found herself tackling each evening like an obstacle course. Could she avoid the Green Room freak with the back-of-the-stalls voice? Don't trip over the actressy actress who had once played opposite a knight and was determined to relive the experience *ad nauseum*. And woe betide her if the famous knight himself made an entrance, he of the wandering eyes and wandering hands. But the *Taro Beach* team and accompanying partners grouped together beneath the clear blue skies were a complete contrast. Unassuming and friendly, they had welcomed her into their midst. There were poseurs, of course. A photographer was going the rounds, and girls in painted-on white suede or skimpy black ciré were taking deep breaths and smiling letter box smiles in the hope of attracting attention, but they were in the minority.

Erin had noticed Jago having his photograph taken with the *femmes fatales*, and had wondered whether Poll or Susie could be numbered amongst their midst. Was Poll the pneumatic blonde with pink bows in her hair? Could the redhead who never stopped laughing be Susie? There was no chance to find out for she was not introduced, though Jago did introduce her to plenty of other people. He was an attentive host, taking care she was not left alone. In expectation of being a member of the persecuted minority she had been grateful, but had quickly realised that no obstacles needed to be avoided here.

'My hips go in and out like a concertina,' sighed the matron beside her, making eyes at a slice of blueberry cheesecake on a nearby plate. 'I swear I have no idea why.'

'Would you cut it out already?' ordered her husband, a cameraman, with mock bombast. 'You spend half your life with your goddamn head stuck in the goddamn fridge.'

'Marvin, I don't!' she squealed.

'Ethel, you do.' He hugged her around the waist. 'That's where all those sexy inches come from, and the more the merrier as far as I'm concerned.'

'Sexy inches?' purred a velvety male voice into Erin's ear. 'The sexiest inches here today belong to you.'

Unimpressed by this opening gambit, she turned to find a young man smiling down at her. Erin had to admit that although his words might not have impressed, his looks did. He had jet black hair, heavy-lidded dark eyes and a tan smoother than bronze. Sharply dressed in black shirt and designer trousers, with a twist of gold chains around his neck, he was a very long way from the boy next door.

'How ya doin', Kiel?' chorused Marvin and Ethel.

'Fine thanks. How are you folks?' He offered Erin a hand and a flawless white smile. 'Kiel Jennings, and you're Miss Brains and Beauty combined.' He gestured to the far side of the pool where Burt Steen was wiggling stubby fingers in a hello. 'I've been hearing all about you.'

'Don't tell me,' she groaned.

'Why not?' The dark eyes smouldered. 'Burt didn't exaggerate.'

She gave a dubious smile and, beneath the ensuing banter, took time to study the new arrival. A 'pretty dude' the agent had said, quoting a melting-pot ancestry of Sicilian-Italian and American-Indian, and there he had not been exaggerating. Kiel Jennings registered high on the breathtaking scale, though he was too perfect, too aware of the impact he made for her taste. Erin's eyes strayed through the crowd to Jago. Casual as always, he was wearing faded jeans and a shirt which had seen other summers. Laughing with friends, he unconsciously rumpled his hair, scattering blond strands across his brow. He was not classically good-looking, yet that inner force gave him ten times the charisma of the young man standing beside her. She much preferred Jago. Erin frowned. *She much preferred Jago*? Where had that thought come from? It sounded disturbingly solid. She switched her eyes back to the group around her, her mind back to Kiel. It was surprising that such a lightweight character possessed the power to make Jago as tense as he had been last weekend. She would have thought Jago more likely to brush off the other actor's fits of pique.

'My will-power's having an off day.' Ethel was ogling the cheesecake again. She linked an arm through her husband's. 'Let's you and me go in search of desserts.'

'Jago's laid on some wonderful food,' Erin praised, as the older couple headed off in the direction of the buffet table.

'Correction, Jago's laid on nothing,' she was informed. 'He might be playing mine host, but the television company's picking up the tab for everything today. Old skinflint Miles'd never splash out on food and drink for damn near a hundred guests.' Kiel's laugh removed most of the sting from the words. Most, not all, she noted. 'This is a promotional shindig to push *Taro Beach* in the press. That's why the photographer's shooting everything which moves.'

Erin shrugged, accepting she did not know the form. 'Well, it's nice of him to open his house and gardens to everyone.'

'Wrong again. This mansion isn't his. It belongs to a contact of Burt's who's off on a world tour. The guy needed someone to keep an eye on his house and staff, and because Burt has always felt cheated that his Numero Uno chose to live in a timber shack, he used that silver tongue of his. Seems the guy's wife went ape at the mention of Jago's name and—hey presto—moving in was a formality. Mind you, I hear Burt needed to give Jago a sharp kick in the pants to get him to agree.' Her companion's gaze fell to the cut crystal tumbler she was holding. 'Can I get you a fresh drink? What was that, gin and orange?'

'Straight orange, but I don't want another one, thanks.' Erin handed her glass to a passing waiter. 'You say Jago lived in a shack?' she enquired.

'Would you believe a rented shack? No, not a shack exactly,' Kiel adjusted, 'but not the kind of place you'd associate with a high roller who pulls in his money. But that's our Mr Miles all over. Doesn't own a house, a boat, not even a car.' Judging from his disgust, not owning a car equated with not owning a toothbrush. 'No wife, no kids, and he's avoided getting soaked for alimony like some of us. The guy has it made. A bachelor in paradise, that's him.' Her partner slid a bronzed hand into a hip pocket to withdraw an aggressively expensive leather-bound cigarette case. 'Smoke?'

'I don't,' she said vaguely, her mind fleeing around these revelations.

'You don't drink, you don't smoke. What do you do?' The dark eyes burned a path from her head to her toes. She was wearing a lavender-pink silk shirt and slacks, but might as well have been wearing cellophane. 'With a body like that I sure hope it's something two can share.'

'I spend most of my time writing. Though I do jog and swim, and things,' Erin added, too busy thinking about Jago and his finances to pay much attention.

' "Things" sound interesting.' Kiel indicated roughly-hewn stone steps at the far corner of the lawn which led down through a grove of palm trees to the ocean. 'Let's go.'

She gazed in surprise at the hand he held out to
her. How had they come this far, this quickly?

'Aren't we supposed to circulate?' she stalled.

'No sweat, we can circulate later. Who's going to
panic if we dodge out for a while?' He put his hand
over hers, linked through his fingers and held on
tight. 'I'd like to see the beach,' he said, pulling her
with him across the grass. 'It's rare I visit this coast,
it's rare any of us do. The studios are on the east,
over a hundred miles away, so I've yet to puzzle out
why Jago chooses to base himself here.'

'The island is very beautiful,' Erin pointed out.

She had decided she would go where Kiel led. So
long as his talk centred on their host she was
interested. Any information about Jago was grist to
her mill and today she was learning a lot.

'Beautiful—pah!' her escort derided. 'All the
action's in Miami. Something's happening over
there twenty-four hours a day. The town's alive with
nightclubs, fancy hotels, restaurants, but what you
got around here?' His lip twisted. 'Not much else
than the Everglades. And what's that—a goddamn
swamp!'

'A swamp teeming with wildlife,' she said,
picking her way down the steps in her high-heeled
sandals.

'You like that kind of stuff?' Kiel demanded.

'Well, I haven't actually been, I've only read the
guide books, but——'

'There you are, you haven't been and who the hell
wants to? No, this coast is dullsville. Jago has to be
crazy to motor across Alligator Alley twice every
day. All he's done is saddle himself with a hefty
chunk of unnecessary travel.'

'Alligator Alley?'

'The two-lane highway which cuts straight across the foot of Florida. Say, how about me picking you up next Sunday and taking you over to Miami?' Kiel suggested, as they walked between the palms. 'You'd get to see Alligator Alley and I could lay on some wildlife.' He grinned suggestively, squeezing her fingers. 'The personal kind. I'm a tiger when I'm aroused and that sexy sway to your hips says you are, too.'

With a sharp tug, Erin freed her hand from his grasp. A little of Kiel Jennings went a long way.

'Sorry, but I'm busy next Sunday,' she told him. 'As you probably know I'm working on a profile on Jago, and——'

'To hell with Jago. I'm asking you out, he never will. Even a beautiful English rose couldn't coax that guy to ease open the purse-strings. Jago never socialises, so don't you get any ideas about being wined and dined.' Kiel had been scowling, but now he switched on the flawless smile. 'Why are we talking about Jago when I'd rather talk about you—us?' In a feat of engineering which must have been honed through years of practice, he slid an arm around her shoulders, steered her from the path and had Erin positioned with her back against a palm tree in seconds. 'You're different,' he said, leaning over her and starting to purr. 'No plastered on goo, no false eyelashes, just a light tan and——' the dark eyes undressed her '— one helluva good body. Skip writing next Sunday,' he appealed. 'You and I can——'

As he leant forward to whisper his intentions into her ear, Erin decided it was time to depart. A speedy evaluation showed he had one hand spread

on the tree trunk above her head, the other beside
her hip. Would a firm shove be the most effective
method of escape, or a quick wriggle under and out?
She selected the wriggle, but had no time to duck for
at that moment a tall figure in faded jeans strode
into the grove.

'Cool it,' said Jago, his hand landing on Kiel's
shoulder. 'Erin isn't up for grabs.'

Surprised, the younger man spun round. When he
saw who had arrived, he bristled. 'Who says I'm
grabbing?' he demanded.

'I see you in action daily. I know your technique,'
Jago replied, in a tone which was not so much
disapproving as faintly incredulous.

Kiel adopted a fighting stance. Bronzed fists
were clenched, the shoulders beneath the black
shirt flexed. 'Do you want to fight?' he threatened.

'No, thank you. Look, there's no need for bully-
boy tactics, so just beat it. Please?'

'You try and make me.'

'Again, no thanks.' Jago sighed. 'All I'm saying is
Erin's out of bounds.'

'Since when?'

'Since now. And put your fists down—please.'

Erin's eyes moved from one man to the other.
Whilst Kiel was menacing, lips stretched back
across his teeth and all ready to fight, Jago's
behaviour was as she would have expected. He was
calm and composed. The other actor was not
upsetting him today. Yet had she decoded an
impatience? If the pseudo-heavyweight reached
back to throw a punch could it be Jago's knuckles
which struck home first?

'Violence isn't the answer to anything,' she
intervened.

Jago slung her a sideways look. 'You mean make love, not war?' Her reply was to nod feverishly. 'Toots, your wish is my command,' he replied.

His arm encircled her waist, his head came down and, to her amazement, he kissed her. Zappo. The immediate pressure of his lips was innocent, but then she felt a movement within him and his mouth parted on hers. His tongue thrust into her mouth, an erotic invader. Startled and utterly captivated, she responded, allowing the kiss to deepen. Blood stormed through her veins like a flash-flood. Dimly Erin was aware she should protest, break free, but a raw sexual need which she could not control was directing her actions. She was paralysed. How did she come to be pressed up against a lean, male body? she wondered. And *this* male body? If Kiel had laid claim minutes earlier, her evasion would have been swift, but to have her mouth plundered by a blond Viking left her clinging to him for support.

Eventually Jago raised his head. 'Well now,' he murmured.

She gazed at him, pleasure, fear, shame, all swirling topsy-turvy inside her. 'What—what do you think you're doing?' Erin managed to gasp, aware her usual decorum, her common sense had let her down miserably. Had she gone temporarily insane?

'Obeying orders.' He directed his attention to Kiel. 'Erin's out of bounds for the simple reason we're ... hot.' His male to male wink conveyed nights filled with debauchery and orgiastic activities. 'We prefer to be discreet and we'd be obliged if you could keep quiet, too.'

'Sure thing.' Because a claim had been actively

staked, Kiel understood. 'I'd never trespass on another man's territory,' he vowed, backing away. 'No hard feelings?'

'None,' he was assured benevolently.

'Thanks.' With a hand raised in farewell, he headed off towards the sounds of the distant barbecue.

'What was that all about?' demanded Erin, pushing all thoughts of *her* co-operation, *her* response, to one side. 'How come you say I'm not up for grabs and promptly grab me yourself?'

'You needed rescuing.'

'I did not!'

'You can't mean——?' Jago shifted his weight on to one leg. 'Are you as green as a fresh dollar bill?' he enquired. 'Surely you can see Kiel's a——'

'I know all about Kiel,' she cut in tartly. 'I may live in a cute little cottage in a cute little village, but I'm not Red Riding Hood. I can recognise a wolf when I see one. I can also recognise being compromised.'

'But I had to rescue you some way. Hell, I'm responsible for you, and a friendly peck on the cheek wouldn't have worked. Kiel doesn't understand subtlety. For him everything needs to be spelled out in capitals.'

'As in H O T?' The letters shot from her lips like pellets from a gun. 'You don't honestly believe he'll keep that piece of news to himself, do you?' Erin demanded. 'My guess is it's going the rounds right now.'

'Could be.'

'Could be?' she spluttered. 'Is that all you have to say? But then, what's another rumour where you're concerned? It just adds a notch to your ladykiller reputation. But what about me? I need a rumour about us—us messing around—like I need a hole in the head. One of the criteria in writing biographies——'

'I thought you were writing a profile? Jago interrupted.

'A profile, but nearly a biography,' she insisted. 'One of the criteria is that the biographer is an observer, someone who makes a detached assessment. How is anyone going to believe my account of you is detached if my name is bandied around as—as——'

'As my lover?' he queried, amusement at her fury showing in the creases at the corners of his mouth. 'Aren't you taking this whole thing much too seriously?'

'No, I'm not. My integrity's at stake here!'

His shoulders rose and fell. 'If you feel that strongly I'll find Kiel and put him straight,' he offered. 'Though it'll mean he's going to consider you are up for grabs. So whatever happens, don't disappear with him into the bushes again. Understand?'

Erin placed her hands on her hips. 'You're missing the point. I can look after myself, thank you very much. I had the situation under complete control, and as for you being responsible for me— you're not!'

Jago shook his head in disbelief. 'That guy's a compulsive chaser, Erin. He eats little girls like you for breakfast.'

'One.' She held up a tapered finger. 'I'm not a little girl, and two.' A second finger came up. 'What about your reputation?'

'Toots, by current standards I'm relatively puritan.'

'A Trappist monk?' she scoffed. 'Sorry, it won't wash. Don't forget I have access to Burt's collection of cuttings.'

'And most feature items he's made up and fed to the press. Yes. Burt insists, and to a point it's true, that for the sake of my career I must appear to be ... adventurous. If I said I stayed home nights and built cathedrals from matchsticks nobody's going to get excited. And in my line, unfortunately, image matters.'

With a sigh she conceded the point, then added, 'But I'd be grateful if in future you'd allow me to handle my life my own way.'

'What you mean, toots, is don't kiss you again. One single kiss is what you're arguing about, isn't it?'

'No!' Erin said indignantly. 'Yes!'

Jago chuckled. 'Come along, I'll introduce you to William.'

Back at the barbecue the *Taro Beach* director, a dapper individual with silver-white hair and a goatee beard, was happy to be taken to one side. When Jago explained who she was and the favour she required, he smiled widely.

'Burt's already filled me in.'

'Don't believe a word,' Erin begged, to the accompaniment of Jago's laughter.

'I imagine after Burt's build-up you can't figure out whether to bow to Erin on bended knee or discuss Einstein's Theory of Relativity?' he teased.

The director nodded, joining in the fun. 'One thing's for sure, I realise we can't afford to miss out on her patronage.' He patted the chair beside him.

'Sit down, sweetheart, and let's you and me talk.'

'Then I'll disappear,' Jago said, glancing at her in such a way she was sorely tempted to stick out her tongue. 'I need to set Kiel right on a thing or two.'

'Why not visit us on location in a couple of weeks?' William suggested, when they ware alone. 'Normally we film around the Miami-Fort Lauderdale area, but a lakeside sequence is planned for this episode. The date's not been finalised, but I'll pass on a message when it is. The location is forty miles or so south of here. You could come down with Jago in the studio limo.'

'Thanks,' Erin said happily. 'That sounds ideal.'

'It'll mean an early start,' the director warned, though not as early as usual for Jago. Damn near two hours travelling at the beginning and end of each day would flatten me. How he stands it, I don't know.' William peered through the crowd, locating their host who had been sidetracked by Ethel and Marvin. 'He's a great guy. Professional to his fingertips. Between you and me, Jago keeps *Taro Beach* alive. But he's doing too much, he needs to take things easier.'

'How? Six days a week and all that travelling make for a gruesome timetable.'

'Five days.'

Erin frowned. 'Five?'

'He never works Wednesdays. He insisted it was written into his contract from the start. Though despite turning in just five days, it's equivalent to six. You don't find Jago fluffing his lines, or complaining the lighting doesn't flatter him, or——' the director searched out Kiel '—or needing time off to comb his hair. I'd like to think Jago rested Wednesdays, but I'm sure he doesn't.'

'Then what does he do?' she enquired, her curiosity on full alert.

William grunted. 'God knows, I don't. I did ask once, but I was told to mind my own goddamn business.'

CHAPTER FOUR

JAGO not only had hidden depths, he was also riddled with subterranean caverns. Over the days which followed, Erin devoted far more time to thinking about what she didn't know about him than what she did. As a man with an inflated salary and none of the usual outgoings, he must be piling up riches, but for what? One explanation could be that after such a raggle-taggle childhood he required the security of dollars in the bank. Yet Jago did not rate his childhood as raggle-taggle, that was strictly her view. Also he appeared steadfastly secure in his own psyche. Next she moved on to the mysterious Wednesdays. Maybe he was a sports fanatic, and had insisted on a mid-week break in order to ride surf or sail? No, that did not ring true either.

These depths and caverns were a challenge. One of the most intriguing aspects of writing biographies was the investigative side, and Erin felt a *frisson* of excitement. What a fillip for her book if she could reveal something totally unexpected!?

The plan must be for her to discover the truth as far as she could and, given it was admissible, persuade Jago to allow her to use it. In the past she had sometimes needed to coax her subjects to agree that certain facts should be, and could be, published, but no one had suffered. No one had regretted being honest, divulging their secrets. What were Jago's secrets? If only she could ask outright what he did with his money and where he went on Wednesdays; but such a frontal attack was impossible. If he had told a long-time colleague such as William to mind his own business, he was not going to respond favourably to a query from her, and Erin had no wish to upset the *status quo*. So far Jago had co-operated in full. Nothing had been declared off-limits, and the longer it stayed that way, the better. The ease between them must be consolidated. Before searching questions could be risked, she needed to accumulate a store of good will.

Ease? Good will? When writing the previous profiles she had had no difficulty in stacking up ease and good will on one side, while maintaining a detached view on the other, but could she do this with Jago? As an observer, her role had experienced an unfortunate blur. Erin sighed. That damned kiss was the blur, it seemed to have put everything ever so slightly out of focus.

'You need a man,' Cleo had once declared when lambasting her for her subdued lifestyle. 'A big, lusty man.'

Recalling the dither she had been reduced to in his arms, she wondered uneasily if this could be true. Certainly ever since, the touch of his lips, the moist warmth of his mouth had been relived in a manner more suited to a moonstruck teenager than a sensible thirty-year-old. Enough, she told herself sharply. Obliterate the kiss. It meant nothing. Erin came to a decision. The minute this book was finished she would take a break, a long break from writing. If she circulated and had more contact with the opposite sex, then surely she would be better able to take maverick kisses in her stride? Her brow creased. No, she wouldn't have time off after this book, it would be after the next one. Another Edwardian biography was already stewing in the back of her mind.

She returned to her current project. The pieces of Jago's life which she held in her hand did not make much sense, but wasn't that often the way? Writing a biography was a slow process, much like constructing a jigsaw. You could build and build, and not see the picture clearly until—click—one piece fitted in and made sense of all the rest. For her book's sake she was obliged to search out that vital piece which meant, she assured herself intently, it was her duty to ask questions.

'I understand Jago doesn't go into the studios on Wednesdays,' she said, when Maria appeared with the afternoon's supply of coffee. 'What does he do?'

'Don't ask me, hon. He just shoots out of here at nine in the morning, and doesn't return until after we've gone at night. I've tried quizzing him, but— zilch. He sure can be tight-lipped when he chooses.' The housekeeper settled a plump hip on the corner of the desk. 'Maybe we shouldn't have done, but the girls and me got Rafael to trail him once. Didn't work out though. The kid followed Jago across the causeway and several miles south, then he lost him. 'Course, Jago goes like the wind.'

'You've no idea where he could've been heading?'

'None. Rafael lost him before a fork in the road. The right-hand route heads towards the Everglades, the left veers inland.' Maria shrugged. 'There's nothing much inland. Farming land mostly, with a few mobile home communities, camp sites, a cemetery and a hospital.'

Wednesday evening found Erin keen-eyed and sharp-eared, looking and listening for clues. Under cover of his reminiscences—Jago had reached his adolescence—she made an inspection. Did he seem less tired, more tired? Invigorated? Depressed? Happier? Sad? Less talkative, more talkative? Frustratingly, he seemed exactly the same. She learned nothing.

But when Poll moved into the bungalow a day later, she did learn something—that it was a mistake to go for the obvious where Jago was concerned. Yes, the girl was young and brown, but she also had short, straight mousy hair, a flat chest and glasses.

'She's a nurse,' Maria reported, perching on the edge of the desk for what had now become a regular mid-afternoon chat. 'Works nights and sleeps most of the day. Doesn't say much. I gather she's moved in here because she's looking for peace and quiet. Too many kids running around in her last neighbourhood.'

'And I thought she was Jago's girlfriend!'

The housekeeper went off into peals of laughter. 'He'd hardly stick her out there if she was, would he? He'd have her in the house with him. But that skinny little Plain Jane and Jago? No, he'd need a whole lot more woman than that to satisfy him.' She giggled. 'I'd put my name forward myself if I didn't know my old man'd kick up a rumpus.'

'Has he had girls living in the house before?' Erin queried.

'Nope. There've been a couple who stayed the night, but it was only a night.' Maria's voice dropped to swapping confidences level. 'I reckon he's pining for that Olivia. They lived together for three years, all lovey-dovey, then split up real sudden. One minute she was there, the next she'd gone, like she fell off the edge of the earth. Sounds fishy to me. I tried to tackle Burt, but he got cagey. Wouldn't meet my eyes. His version is Jago lost interest, but the girls and me figure it must have been the other way around. You only have to read the magazines to know the guy was smitten. He took Olivia everywhere, made sure she had her share of the limelight. 'Course Burt would never admit Jago could get dropped like a hot potato, same as anyone else.' The housekeeper sighed. 'That Olivia must have been crazy. When she dropped him she dropped a gorgeous fella. Hadn't you better drink your coffee, hon? It'll be getting cold.'

Amassed wealth? Hush-hush Wednesdays? And now a question mark against Olivia's name. With Jago nothing was straightforward.

Although his account of his childhood was interesting, Erin was relieved when the end of the week brought an end to that portion of his life. His younger years represented the *hors d'oeuvre*, but in his adult life she was being offered a course she could really get her teeth into.

'So another episode begins,' Jago remarked, as they settled down the following Monday evening. He placed the toe of one foot against the heel of the other and eased off a sneaker, then repeated the process with the other shoe. 'Aren't you bored with listening to me rattling on?'

'Aren't you bored with rattling on and me listening?' she countered.

He smiled his crinkle-eyed smile. 'Oddly enough I'm enjoying it—sort of. Usually I detest interviews, all that hokum about am I involved with my leading lady.' Jago stretched out his legs and wiggled his bare toes. 'But speaking to you is—therapeutic. Like going to a shrink, but cheaper.'

This mention of finance seemed to open the door to a pertinent question.

'Did you go into acting because of the money?'

'Go into a high risk business like this for cash? Give me a break. Have you any idea of the percentage of the acting profession who are unemployed at any one time?' He rolled his eyes in horror. 'No, I went into acting by chance, and because I didn't possess qualifications to do much else. All the moving around as a kid loused up my formal education and thus my career prospects. No way could I become an attorney or an engineer. As it happened I was friendly with a guy who helped make TV commercials, and he said that with my hair he could find me work.' Jago grinned, flicking dismissively at a tawny-blond wing. 'If I go bald it's oblivion for me. I did a couple of commercials, one of which was seen by a producer. He required a Scandinavian type for a play he was setting up and before I knew it I was——' He waggled his fingers to denote quotation marks '— an actor.'

'Sounds easy.'

'It was.' His expression stilled. 'Sometimes I lie awake nights feeling guilty because I've never starved or slogged my way through drama school. But maybe I'll be forced to atone later, who knows?'

'You mean if *Taro Beach* finishes you could have difficulty in . . .'

'Why should *Taro Beach* finish?' he interjected, his tone becoming flinty. 'Soap operas go on for years.'

'Not all of them,' Erin demurred. 'And according to the newspaper I read this morning *Taro Beach* has dropped a point or two in the ratings.'

'A hiccup,' he said, and lifted a packet of cigars.

'Why did you join *Taro Beach* in the first place?'

Okay, she accepted the question was premature, but if Jago continued relating his tale at an even pace they would not reach his soap opera debut for another week, and her curiosity refused to sit in a corner and wait that long.

'Do I detect veiled criticism?' In what seemed slow motion, he selected a cheroot, lit it, inhaled, exhaled. 'I joined because the money was great, the people friendly, and the place right. Florida has a wonderful climate. It's not called the Sunshine State for nothing. I guess the accusation is I sacrificed my art for dollars, but——' the blue eyes which met hers were steady '— as a career move it made a lot of sense.'

'Did it?'

His explanation sounded reasonable, yet Erin remained unconvinced. Even if the soap opera did attract hordes of followers, it was still trash. Watching an episode at the motel, she had felt that a teenybopper scribbling on the back of an envelope would have been capable of producing a more sparkling plot. Admittedly Jago had given a good performance, at times he had even managed to lift the banal story into the realms of realism, but a good career move? She thought not. Or were her own prejudices getting in the way? If you acted well, did it really matter whether you acted before an élitist middle-class audience who had paid money to sit in a theatre, or before the masses who lounged at home in front of a flickering screen? Erin gave a mental shrug.

'But why do you live so far away from the studios?' she questioned.

'Because I prefer this coast to the other. Non-stop concrete does nothing for me. Also if I went out on the streets in Miami there's the chance I'd be mobbed, but on the island people respect my privacy. I can go around here like a normal person—almost.' Jago pulled on his cigar. 'Have you had much of a look at the island yourself?'

'Not yet.'

'You must. Why don't I take you on a tour next Sunday?' he suggested.

'Er, I was intending to type up some of our conversations then,' Erin waffled, thrown into sudden confusion.

She had presumed all future contact would be within a working environment, and was unsure of the wisdom of deviating from this pattern. Would it serve any purpose in terms of the profile? Building up good will was important, but . . . In spite of all her self-denials, the memory of his kiss continued to haunt her and she had noticed a propensity in her to be overly aware of Jago as a very attractive male.

'The excursion won't take long, the island's not that big.' A grin tugged at his mouth when he saw her reluctance. 'Doesn't all work and no play make Erin a dull girl?'

Her chin lifted. 'I'd love to come.'

'Great, I'll pick you up around two. Now, back to the grindstone. In that first play I was more or less just a spear carrier, but in the next——'

Erin changed her clothes three times before finally

settling on pale soda-pink garage mechanic-type overalls. A pink chiffon band was tied around her head, then untied then tied again. She did not want to look too studiedly dressed, yet at the same time she wanted to look a little bit special. She baulked at defining why. Maybe it was because those girls who had posed with Jago at the barbecue had been glitzy creatures, and she needed to prove she could give them a run for their money? She grimaced at herself in the mirror. With big brown eyes, short straight nose and a generous mouth, she was not bad looking herself. Add false eyelashes a foot long, and she'd be a glamour puss.

When she ventured out into the sunshine at two o'clock, there was no sign of Jago. Then a horn blared. Erin looked round to see a man on a motorbike, a beat-up old motorbike, raising a hand in salute. He was wearing an ancient white T-shirt, brown cords, a flat cap and dark glasses. She blinked and approached with cautious steps.

'It's you,' she said stupidly.

'Who else?'

'But——'

She gazed at him in dismay. Jago intended to take her a tour of the island on a motorbike? But she had never been on a motorbike before. Too late she remembered Kiel saying he didn't own a car, and at the same time Maria's comment on him 'going like the wind' reverberated.

'Do I look that bad?' he asked with a grin. 'Don't worry, I'll dispense with the disguise once we're out of town. It's just that in the vicinity of the motel there's a danger of bumping into fans, and I'd prefer not to be recognised.' He touched the peak of the cap. 'It's amazing how effective this is at changing the shape of my face.'

'I don't mind the cap, it's—it's——' Erin's eyes drank in the motorbike. It looked fearsomely big and powerful.

'Sorry my steed's short on polished chrome,' he said, continuing to pick up the wrong vibes, 'But the engine's been souped up, so it does go.' To prove his point Jago adjusted the throttle, and the bike roared like thunder.

She gave a thin smile. 'I believe you.'

'Hop on.'

At this point the sensible thing would have been to confess she was a greenhorn where motorbikes were concerned, but instead she took a deep breath and gamely swung her leg across the pillion.

'Here.' He reached back to take hold of her arms and wrap them around his waist. 'Hold on tight,' he cautioned.

Erin held on tight. Very tight. She jammed herself up against him, her breasts flattened against the solid wall of his back. The name of the game was togetherness. They shot away from the kerb with her clinging on for dear life. Her heart thumped staccato. It seemed at least a mile before she dared draw breath. At first she couldn't work out where to put her head—her chin was jammed up against his shoulderblades—then her legs caused problems.

'There's the marina,' Jago shouted over his shoulder, as a dock decorated with bobbing white boats whizzed by. 'That's the sailing club and——' he pointed '— that's a great restaurant for sea food. Their fresh stone crabs are delicious.' As he spoke his hand was waving around in emphasis. Erin wished very much he would put it back on the handlebars. 'Over there's the riding school, and in a minute or so we'll come to one of the golf courses. The island has three.'

'Nice,' she gulped, hearing her voice sound thin and wavery But at least it was a response. She had not uttered a word since they had left the motel, and Jago's running commentary was for her benefit. It was time she contributed.

'We're heading out of town, if you can call it a town,' he yelled, the words blowing back to her ears on the warm wind. 'This is where the unspoiled part of the island begins. From here on it's bays, beaches, lagoons, and most of them deserted. Great, isn't it?'

'Great,' she cried, hoping he wouldn't turn and see the strained expression on her face.

They skirted the golf course, skimmed around a lagoon, left the town behind, and in time her panic began to ease. Jago might drive fast, but as far as she could tell his handling of the bike was faultless. They made a long uphill climb, their speed reducing, then crested the peak and swept down.

'Corner ahead,' he warned.

In preparation Erin tensed her thighs and tightened her grip around his waist. He was firm and solid, she could feel hard muscles moving beneath his skin. The corner meant they tipped at an angle, but instead of being scared she was unexpectedly exhilarated. Emerging on to the straight, she wanted to chuckle. She had managed fine. Riding a motorbike was not that difficult, after all. She began to understand why Jago was so obviously an addict. To be speeding along with the hot air bombarding your body felt invigorating, adventurous, heady. Erin discovered she was enjoying herself. The wind was rippling through her hair, the sun was warm on her back, and the power of the machine beneath her was intoxicating.

Jago shouted something she couldn't catch, but whatever he'd said, he was laughing. She started to laugh, too. This was great stuff. Like a child let out of school, she sat behind him, a grin plastered all over her face.

There was hardly any traffic, and the island proved to be as unspoilt as he had promised. Clean of hamburger joints and funfairs, all she saw were one or two people stretched out on the sand or collecting shells. Yachts with red sails, white sails, yellow sails, rode the waves.

'Fancy a crack at the Rally of the Pharaohs?' Jago called.

She strained to hear. 'The what?'

'Rally of the Pharaohs.'

Erin did not know what he meant, but when he swung off the road and on to a trail which wove its way between desultory palm-trees towards rolling dunes, she began to understand. Kicking up sand and stones, they bounced along. Bump—bump—bump. Erin's breath might be being pounded out of her, her balance precarious, but the grin remained in place.

'Okay?' shouted Jago.

'Okay.'

He reached round and patted her back. 'Good girl.'

Erin laughed out loud. She hadn't had so much fun for ages, years even. Barely aware of what she was doing, she snuggled closer, her cheek against his shoulder. She liked being glued to him, liked his strength, his masculinity. He was an easy man to lean on.

'Jago,' she said, deciding it was time he realised she was a novice rider. 'I have a confession to make.'

'Can't hear you.'

They were almost at the sand hills and now he throttled back, reducing their speed.

'I have a confession to make,' she began again, pulling back to reposition herself. As she moved, Erin's glance fell. His T-shirt had come adrift from his trousers, and she saw a strip of tanned skin—smooth skin, gleaming with health. Would he be tanned all over?

'You have a what?'

In turning his head to catch her answer Jago didn't see the stray boulder, half hidden in the sand. Donk! There was a fierce double bump. He swerved, the machine jerked, shuddered and freewheeled amongst the dunes. Somewhere along the way Erin toppled off while Jago and the bike continued on. Winded, she lay on the slope where she had fallen. She wasn't hurt, they hadn't been going fast enough for that, and when she thought how adroitly she and the bike had parted company, she wanted to giggle. She had shot off in one direction, it had kept going in another. Very neat. Very smooth. Like something out of a Twenties slapstick comedy. She lifted her head and looked around. Jago was nowhere in sight, but noises beyond the curve of sand told her he had also fallen off and was now scrambling to his feet.

'You okay, Erin?' he called. 'I'll be with you in a minute. I've lost my damn glasses and——' She heard him scuffle about. 'Got them!'

High above the sun dazzled, and Erin closed her eyes. Then a grin spread. Jago had tricked her with that kiss, but wasn't trickery a game two could play? She removed the grin, arranged herself in a suitably rag doll position, and lay still. She heard him approach. He was pushing the bike.

'Erin?' he said. It was difficult to keep her face straight, but she managed. 'Erin?' he said again, cautiously this time 'Oh my God, Erin!' The bike thudded to the sand. He dropped to his knees beside her. His shadow fell, cutting out the sun's glare.

She opened her eyes and smiled. 'Boo,' she said.

'You bitch! You silly little bitch!'

Her smile froze. Jago was leaning over her, his face contorted with rage. The joke had misfired.

'Jago, I——' she began.

'You think that's funny?' he blasted. 'You think pretending to be hurt's funny? Well, it's not. It's irresponsible and childish and downright cruel.'

She pushed herself up on to one elbow. 'I only——'

'You have a warped sense of humour, do you know that?'

His nostrils were flared, his eyes as cold as icebergs. 'Let's give Jago the fright of his life. Ha, bloody ha!'

Erin recoiled. His fury would have been comic if it had not been so real.

'I'm sorry.'

'Sorry, sorry? Is this the way you get your kicks, making other people suffer? What do you do for an encore?' he demanded. 'Splash tomato ketchup over yourself?'

'I've said I'm sorry.'

'Big deal.' Jago glared at her from beneath the peak of his cap. 'I've heard of sick jokes, but this has to be the sickest, the dumbest, the——'

'Stop it!' She sat up straight. 'And calm down. What's got into you? I was only teasing. There's no need to go on and on.'

He peeled off the cap to run a large hand through his mane of blond hair. 'No, no there's not,' he sighed, his anger collapsing. 'I guess I'm over-reacting. Forgive me. It's just——' There was a fraught pause, and when his blue eyes met hers she glimpsed a pain inside. 'It's just that the last time I saw a girl lying like that, her head to one side, her limbs disjointed, she wasn't teasing. It was for real. We'd been driving along and this fool in a pick-up truck came out of nowhere, and——' His face seized up.

'Jago.' Her hand flew to his arm, to touch and comfort. 'I had no idea. I'm terribly sorry.'

He gave an embarrassed laugh. 'It's not your fault, it's mine. I never realised how close my emotions are to the surface. I thought I'd put memories of the crash behind me, but seeing you like that triggered them off again.' He paused, tracing an aimless pattern in the sand. 'I don't know why it should. You look nothing like——'

'Like who?' Erin enquired. Her biographer's antennae had been sensitised. There was information to be had, if only she could coax it out of him.

Jago brushed the sand from his hands. 'Like no one. Let's pretend this never happened, okay?' Everything was being put back into a box and the lid firmly closed. 'What say you we leave the bike here and stroll down to the sea?'

'Sounds like a good idea, ' she agreed, having no alternative but to accept that he had eluded her. Using his arm as leverage, Erin stood up. 'On your feet,' she said, when he sat there.

Jago held up his hand and grinned. 'I'm not as agile as you. This old man needs assistance.'

'You forget, I'm the one who's too old and too pale,' she said drolly.

His eyes swept over her. 'You're developing a great tan, and as far as the age bit goes—I'd had a bad night when you woke me up and I was cranky. I'm only human,' he cajoled, adopting an air of pained innocence. 'Help me.'

'Erin obliged by grabbing hold of his wrist with both hands and pulling for all she was worth. He never budged an inch.

'Ever heard of the word "co-operate"?' she panted, her cheeks growing pink.

'Yes, and I am.'

'You're not.' She was leaning back on her full weight, her sandalled feet sinking deeper and deeper into the sand. 'You rogue, this is no contest. You must be four or five stone heavier than me.'

'Suppose I strip off, would that help?' Jago enquired, and zing, zing, zing—the air was electric. A series of neon dots flashed and twinkled, transmitting themselves from his eyes to hers.

'It wouldn't make any difference,' she replied, wishing he wouldn't look at her like that, for the blue eyes beneath the blond brows had a disturbing intensity.

'It would make a hell of a lot of difference, toots. Heave!' he encouraged.

'You heave, instead of sitting there like a great big—tondo.'

'Who's a tondo?'

'You are. Now, get up,' Erin demanded, tugging on his arm like a mad thing.

He did as he was told. He raised his backside a

few inches from the sand and hovered. They were
like people at a crucial point in a tug of war, using
his arm as the rope. She was at one end, he weighted
down the other. Erin's feet spread, dividing right
and left until she was halfway to doing the splits.
She wobbled. Jago sat down with a thud. She lost
her balance. He jerked his arm, and she wound up
sprawled on top of him.

'Shall I strip now?' he enquired, smiling into the
flushed face inches above his.

'No, thank you.' Did he know the way her blood
was racing? Could he feel the uneven bump of her
heart? 'Behave yourself,' Erin said, uncertain just
who needed the reprimand.

'Why?' His arms tightened around her waist,
binding her to him. On the bike she had been glued
to his back, now she felt as if she was glued to every
inch of him. Glued to every inch of six foot three of
male virility. Was it heaven or was it hell?
Whatever it was, it was not conducive to a detached
assessment. His smile spread. 'Kiss me,' he
requested.

'Jago!' She attempted to escape, but quickly
stopped. Squirming around on top of him was
having a disastrous effect.

'Feel what you've done to me?' he murmured.
'How could you?'

Easily, it seemed.

'Let me go.'

As a demand, it sounded suspiciously like a plea.
What had happened to the unflappable Erin Page?
For years she had been the woman in charge,
always serene, always controlled, and here she was
metamorphosed into a quivering length of flush-
faced, tumbled-haired confusion.

'Not until you've kissed me. It won't hurt.' Jago was smiling that smile which had drawn 'oohs' and 'ahs' from a million fans and which was now drawing something—she dared not think what— from her. 'You liked it last time, remember?'

'I didn't.'

'Now, Erin,' he chided. 'Credit me with some intelligence. It was obvious you found me ... *simpatico*.'

'You're wrong,' she protested, placing a hand on either side of his head and pushing up against the sand. He allowed her to rise, but only inasmuch as she hovered head and shoulders above him.

'I'm not wrong.'

'You are.' Erin strove for dignity, which was tricky, considering her position. 'I'm your biographer, not——'

'Not a would-be bedmate?' Jago cut in, grinning.

'Precisely.'

'I do love that haughty air of yours,' he chuckled. 'It's a real turn-on.'

'Jago, in my kind of writing one of the rules is that——'

'Who cares about a crummy rule? Can't you stop thinking about that book of yours for once and simply follow your instincts?' He moved one hand from her waist and brought it up to cup her breast. 'You're a beautiful, sensual woman,' he said softly, his thumb brushing across a nipple which sprang to rigidity beneath the thin pink cotton. 'You shouldn't be scared of that sensuality, Erin. It's a wonderful gift. Enjoy it.'

Enjoy her sensuality? It was a wonderful gift? She felt the beginnings of hysterical laughter. Jago had everything twisted the wrong way around.

'No I won't. I mustn't! I mean—can't we go down to the sea?' she wailed, and collapsed on top of him as her arms gave way.

'What is it that worries you?' he asked, sliding his hand out from between them. 'Me as the actor, me as the man, or sex itself? But on the bike back there you were rubbing yourself up against me and cooing, so——'

'I was not!'

'Why the hang-up? I want you. With my glands so obviously rampant there's no way I can say otherwise, so why not admit you want me? It's not a crime. We're both free and single, the sky is blue, the birds are singing, God's in his heaven, so?' Jago was watching her closely. 'Have you ever made love outdoors?'

'Don't,' she pleaded. 'Please don't.'

'Always in bed with the lights switched off? What a waste.'

'Jago, let me go.' She bucked and bristled, desperate to get free, but his arms tightened around her.

'After you've kissed me.'

What else could she do? Erin aimed for his cheek, but at the last moment he moved his head which meant her lips collided with his. A hand left her waist to mesh amongst the rich dark curls at the back of her head, and she was held in place. His kiss was dynamite. It blew her apart. His mouth opened beneath hers and Erin found herself participating in an embrace which made any other embrace seem like a pale imitation of the real thing. Her body heat soared. Jago was exploring her mouth, tasting her, then nibbling. He captured first her upper lip between his, and then the lower, again and again

until inside she felt as sweet and soft as a dewdrop.
When he finally stopped, she did not know whether
to laugh or cry.

'There,' he murmured. 'Together we could press
all the right buttons, ring all the right chimes, if you
gave us a chance. You may go now,' he said, when
she continued to lie on top of him like a beached
whale.

Erin scrambled to her feet and began a fastidious
brushing off of her clothes. Inside she squirmed. He
had been seducing her and she had loved it. Just as
she had loved Ned's seduction! Head down,
refusing to meet his eyes in case he was laughing at
her, she went with him to the water's edge. A soft
breeze teased chestnut wisps from her brow, lifted
strands of dark hair from her shoulders. Gradually
her composure seeped back.

'Talk to me,' Jago requested, as they strolled
along, leaving footprints behind them in the wet
sand.

'What about?'

'You '

'There's not much to tell.'

'Don't be evasive.'

'I'm not.' She gave him a brief résumé of her
childhood. 'See, it's all very dull compared to your
experiences.'

'It's all very secure. Go on.' Her teenage and
university years lasted until they reached a tumble
of rocks at the far end of the bay. 'If you studied
history how come you're writing books?' Jago
asked, when they turned to walk back.

'At Oxford I specialised in the Edwardian era
and one of my projects was an actor—manager,'
Erin explained. 'I went through his life with a fine-

tooth comb and discovered some facts which hadn't come to light before. When my tutor read what I'd written, he suggested he approach an agent on my behalf to see if a biography would be of interest. The agent was Cleo. She said yes. I graduated, the book was published and, much to my surprise, the critics liked it. Patrice Lanham——'

'The actress?'

'That's right. She read the biography and asked Cleo if I'd be interested in writing about her.' Erin stuck her hands in her pockets and paced along. 'I wasn't. I'd already had an idea for a book on contemporary women, but they were intended to be women in the street. Writing froth to boost someone's ego held no appeal. However, Cleo has a flair at twisting arms and Patrice was included. The profile on her was——' she pulled a face '— okay. Some froth but also a chunk of information about her work in the theatre. Mind you, if I wrote it again it would be very different,' Erin muttered, then, wary of having sounded vengeful, added with a smile, 'There are always things I want to change when my work appears in print and it's too late.'

'That's the way it goes. When I see myself on the screen I invariably kick myself for not having done better.' Jago frowned, rubbing his chin. 'From what you've said, I take it the book on women was written several years back?'

She nodded. 'I've done three Edwardian biographies since.'

'But why the gap? Why wasn't this book on men a straight follow on? Given a success, the usual procedure is to take advantage and deliver more of the same.'

Erin inspected the horizon. 'Well, I didn't.'

'You mean after the women book you promptly turned tail, retreated from the real world and buried yourself in history again?'

His words were random, yet he had described what she had done with eerie exactitude. She knew there had to be a way of rebuffing what sounded almost a condemnation, but for the moment it escaped her. Then she remembered a snatch of something he had said.

'As a career move it made a lot of sense,' she retaliated.

Hearing his own words thrown back at him, Jago's eyes hardened. If she hadn't fully believed his justification, it was clear he also did not believe hers. He seemed ready to protest, then thought better of it. An awkward silence fell between them.

'What about your marriage?' he asked abruptly.

Erin sighed. 'It was short and sweet, and now it almost seems as though it happened to someone else. Peter and I were married a year or so after I came down from Oxford. Everyone in the village came to our wedding, the little church was packed. It was packed again nine months later—for Peter's funeral. He had leukaemia.'

'That was rough,' Jago murmured, his fingers fleetingly touching her arm.

His sympathy brought an unexpected mist to her eyes, and she blinked.

'Yes. We'd known each other all our lives, yet our actual time together was over in the blink of an eye.' She stared into space.

'Who has there been since? I know you live alone, but I can't believe you've been left alone. A host of young hopefuls are bound to have beaten a path to your door.' He cast her a glance. 'Who?'

Erin went still inside. Somehow this 'talk to me' had turned into a full scale investigation. She felt herself under siege. Jago was expecting names to be named. And why not? she thought contrarily. A name wasn't much. It wouldn't mean anything to him.

'Ned, and—and one or two others,' she said. She had striven to sound offhand, but it didn't work. She knew it didn't work. Terrified he might look into her face and see the whole sordid story written there, she gabbled off in a totally different direction. 'Has a date been set for shooting the lakeside sequence of *Taro Beach*? William said he'd give due warning, but I haven't heard a word.'

'Damn, I'm sorry. I clean forgot.' Jago bounced a palm off his brow in punishment. 'He asked me to tell you it's been fixed for next Tuesday. I also forgot to say I'm flying to New York on Wednesday. I'll be away eight full days. A shoot up there has been off and on for ages, but the guys who control the budget suddenly sanctioned it. I know it'll mess up your schedule and I apologise, but——'

'I am flexible,' she smiled.

'Good.' He paused. 'About the——'

'Race you to the bike,' Erin challenged suddenly, fearful he was restarting his questions about the men in her life.

She leapt forward as if from starting blocks and galloped across the sand. Surprise gave her the advantage, and for the first fifty yards or so she was in the clear, then Jago drew level. He overtook her, went way beyond, using easy, loping strides. He shouted back, laughing, telling her not to be a tortoise, then disappeared from sight into the dunes. When she panted up she found him beside the bike, ostentatiously patting away a yawn.

'Never mentioned my Olympic gold medal for the sprint, did I?' he drawled.

'Must have slipped your mind,' Erin gulped, catching her breath. 'I have to admit that for an old man you can still move.'

He thwacked her on the backside. 'Less lip, junior. you'd be surprised what this old man can still do.' He raised his eyebrows, as if to allow time for the thought to sink in, then began feeling in his pockets.

'If you're looking for your spectacles, you put them in that pannier thing,' she told him.

'Did I? Thanks.' Jago started to unbuckle the worn leatherette container. 'Talking about the Lanham woman, which we aren't but we were, I remember some guy once told Olivia she reminded him of a young Patrice.'

'Was she flattered?' Erin enquired drily.

He grinned. 'Thrilled to bits. Treated the remark as a prophecy she'd become a beldame of the theatre.'

'With regard to Olivia,' she said, deciding this mention of his girlfriend was too good an opportunity to be missed. 'With regard——' She stopped, uncertain how to proceed. Discussing Jago's childhood and career was one thing, discussing a live-in lover was another. 'Er—did the two of you ever join up on stage?'

He had found the spectacles and now he slid them on to his nose. 'No.'

'Why not? Was the idea never mooted?'

Jago rammed on his cap, jerking the peak down over his eyes. 'On the subject of Olivia, I'm not prepared to talk. She's a closed chapter. You may use what's already appeared in print, but understand I'm adding nothing.'

Erin gazed at him. 'You don't mean—you can't mean you're not going to talk about her *at all*?'

'Not a word. I did say certain subjects were off-limits and you agreed it was a deal,' he reminded her.

'I never expected this kind of a veto to be slapped down,' she snorted. 'You and Olivia were together for three years. That's a long time. You can't pretend she never happened.' Erin saw what had promised to be a wonderful profile begin to slide away from her. 'You have to give me something,' she insisted.

'I don't have to give anything.'

'Yes, you do. I'm writing——'

'You're writing a book that's all, not the damned Declaration of Independence.' His voice was clipped. The eyes behind the dark lenses had built a barrier to hold her off. 'A book which'll keep the reader amused for an hour or two, not change the axis the world spins on.'

Erin glared. How dare he talk of her work in such a feckless fashion? Why must he make it sound so—trivial?

'You can't expect me to slap a dollop of recycled material from gossip columns bang in the middle of a first-hand account. That's ridiculous.' Her voice had shrilled, and she needed to make a conscious effort to lower it. 'The entire profile would be rendered null and void.'

'Nonsense.'

'It's not!' she flared. 'Can't you understand how important it is the profile should be authentic?'

'It will be authentic,' Jago replied irritably.

'How, if a portion's just stuff which has been laundered? I think you're being unrealistic.'

He thrust her an icy look. 'And I think you're being too damned pushy. I said no Olivia and I meant no Olivia, so I'd be obliged if you would kindly get off my back and stay off!'

CHAPTER FIVE

ERIN glanced from between thick black lashes. It was early Tuesday morning, and she and Jago were in the rear of a plush limousine, being driven southwards at speed. Her companion's head was resting back and his eyes were closed. He appeared to be asleep. It was a pretence. In reality he was shutting her out, putting space between them as he had done since their argument two days ago—and the reason was Olivia.

After such a promising collaboration everything had been thrust back to square one. Ease? Good will? They seemed vain hopes. Although Jago had talked the previous evening he had been stilted; his dislike of interviews and interviewers resurrected. And in response Erin once more floundered amongst her original misgivings. She had suspected 'off-limits' could be translated as 'problems'. She had suspected correctly. Accuse her of being pushy he might, but didn't her profile give her the right to press for facts? Yes. Why couldn't he see that? Erin chewed at her lip. She supposed there was one consolation in this upheaval, that he would not be kissing her again. Yet as a silver lining it seemed oddly tarnished.

Adding two and two together, it had not been difficult to deduce that Olivia must be dead. She had been the girl lying with limbs disjointed after their car had crashed. Erin could understand why

Jago blenched from talking about her and sympathised, but wasn't he being too extreme? Although the
cuttings had contained no report of any accident,
she had pinpointed Olivia's demise at more than
two and a half years ago, when all mention of her
had ceased. Surely after such a span of time he
should have come to terms?

She gazed through the tinted window. Sunday's
veto had prompted her to read and re-read every
word she could find on the actress. Erin had been
searching, though for what she did not know. Did a
common denominator exist between Olivia, the
mysterious Wednesdays and Jago hoarding his
money? If so, it was not to be found amongst the
press cuttings, though a couple of interesting facts
did emerge.

The first was that Jago had devoted considerable
effort to promoting his girlfriend's career—and to
no avail. Indeed, several snide comments indicated
he would have used his time more profitably if he'd
gone fishing. Erin could only agree. Admittedly the
girl was decorative, in a starlet kind of way, but in
talent she must have been sorely lacking, for despite
Jago's help all she had achieved were walk-on parts,
infrequent ones at that. A future beldame of the
theatre? Not in a million years.

The second fact which shone clear was that when
Olivia had been around Jago had socialised in
plenty. His hot little hand had not clutched the
purse-strings tight in those days. There were
photographs of them at the kind of expensive
restaurants where celebrities congregate, together
at first nights, patronising trendy nightclubs; all
with his girlfriend smiling brightly into the camera.

She had had no inhibitions about being caught as the shutter clicked, nor in providing a comment for the press, which made Jago's stonewall silence all the more frustrating.

Recalling his response to her playing dead at the beach, Erin's stomach churned. She felt dreadful. Yet if nothing else the incident had made her aware of the hurt which he allowed to fester deep inside. Such a private hurt was an unhealthy hurt. A self-destructive hurt. She did not expect him to forget Olivia—she had not forgotten Peter and never would—but Jago needed to cauterise his wound. Two and a half years was long enough to bleed, and until the bleeding stopped he would never be able to build a new life. He urgently needed to work through his feelings, bring them out into the open. Erin frowned, thinking how he had said talking to her was therapeutic. What better therapy could there be than talking about Olivia? And why not face his loss square-on by agreeing to it being mentioned—fleetingly, sensitively—in the profile? How she wished she could persuade him, but that veto had sounded so *final*.

Her brown eyes clouded. There was always the possibility she might be on the wrong track altogether. Maybe Jago's silence could be attributed more to career reasons than to emotional ones? Could the motivation in keeping quiet about Olivia be coldbloodedly a fear of his image being spoiled? Jago had been in the car at the time of the crash, so the chances were his hands had been on the wheel. The driver of the pick-up truck sounded to have been solely at fault, but even so was he afraid of his popularity plummeting if his involvement in Olivia's death became common knowledge? The public could be fickle with their heroes. Uncharacteristic though it seemed, did self-interest reign supreme? Erin shivered, unhappy with her thoughts. Was that why all mention of the crash had been kept out of the newspapers? She turned to frown. What went on inside Jago's head and inside his heart?

He must have sensed her look, for he opened his eyes and spoke. 'Another twenty minutes and we'll be there. The road splits just ahead. We keep right, but if you went left you'd be en route for the area where I lived when I first came to Florida. It's peaceful down there.'

As he closed his eyes, Erin undertook some rapid computations. The fork must be the one Maria had mentioned, and now she would have bet money on Jago having headed left. Cogs turned. Think, girl, think. He had been returning to familiar ground because . . . because there was a cemetery? Because Olivia lay buried in that cemetery? Was it possible Jago had set one day a week aside in order to kneel at the grave of his beloved? Icy fingers clutched at her heart. What a poignant vigil. No, what a *morbid* vigil. Jago was too young to spend the rest of his life looking over his shoulder, constantly grieving.

She must be wrong. Or was it that she wanted to be wrong? Could her own feelings be obscuring the issue? If only she had remained a step removed she would have been able to see Jago in a cool, clear light, but those kisses, those *shared* kisses, had added an extra dimension. Because she found the idea of him being so tightly bound to Olivia unwelcome, that did not mean it could not be true. People do do these things, he had once said. And people did devote themselves to the dead. Hadn't the Emperor Shah Jehan built the magnificent Taj Mahal in remembrance of his wife, Mumtaz Mahal? The icy fingers bit deeper. Jago had been to India, and at an impressionable age. Had he visited the white marble mausoleum? Was his money being used to keep Olivia's memory alive? Not in the building of a tomb, but maybe in some other way?

The idea was too bizarre. However much he bled, Olivia was not an obsession. Proof lay in his interest in other women, his interest in *her*. But was that proof? Men had a different make-up from women, and could involve themselves in physical intimacy whilst remaining emotionally unmoved. Could his attraction to her be physical, full stop?

The thought caught at her throat, made it difficult to breathe. That all she represented to Jago was a female shape equipped with the necessary curves and fissures made Erin feel wretched, yet why not? Ned had viewed her in that way. He hadn't given a damn about the woman who lived inside the body. And if Jago's attraction was similar, then his affections could continue to belong to his dead lover.

The driver turned off the main road. They sped along a track which led into a flat green landscape. On both sides were shallow lakes, where saw-grass sprouted in tufts. Despite the sun above and the blue sky reflected in the water, the Everglades had a desolate air, and the cypress trees which rose from the swamp like bald grey posts emphasised this melancholy.

'If you go exploring, stick to the boardwalk,' Jago warned, coming awake. 'And watch out for alligators. The Seminole Indians do wrestle them barehanded, but——' he arched a brow '— it is a knack.'

'Are there many alligators?' Erin asked, looking warily out at the marsh.

'Ten thousand or so, but as the Everglades cover over a million acres they're thinly spread. I believe there are also five hundred crocodiles, but they prefer sandy beaches and salt water so there shouldn't be any around here.'

'Which means if a jaw fastens itself on my arm I can rest assured it'll belong to an alligator?'

'If a jaw fastens itself on your arm you can rest assured it'll belong to a mosquito,' Jago replied. 'Don't go anywhere until I've rounded up repellent.'

A picnic ground had been requisitioned for the day and here, beside a lake of grass, the limousine came to rest. The people of the *Taro Beach* unit were already gearing themselves up for action, and Erin looked around, fascinated by the clutter of cameras, cables, lights and people. To one side stood a large trailer which was to do duty as dressing-room and make-up booth, and Jago vanished inside. When he re-emerged, he was brandishing a can of insect spray. Her legs were covered in scarlet pants, but a skimpy white cotton top left her arms bare and vulnerable. Not for long, for Jago set to work, painting her down like a subway wall.?

'You should be okay now,' he said, pushing the cap back on to the can. 'William reckons it'll be another half hour before we're ready, so if you want to reconnoitre now's your chance. But keep your eyes open.'

Erin touched her brow. 'Yes, sir.'

A boardwalk led from the picnic ground into the marsh, and she set off. She did keep her eyes open, and when she stopped to peer down between the wooden slats, she was rewarded. Shoals of silver fish glided in patches of clear water, a frog croaked on a submerged log. She did not see any reptiles, but she did take note of what, according to her guidebook, could only be an anhinga, a bird-type creature which swam under water with its snake-like neck protruding. Up in the air, silhouetted against the china blue of the sky, an egret, or was it a heron? fluttered. The half an hour disappeared in no time, and Erin arrived back to watch the first of the two scenes planned for the day being organised.

The action sounded simple. An airboat, a flat-bottomed contraption powered by a huge airplane propeller, was to skim across the lake towards camera and stop at a wooden jetty. Jago, Kiel and a young blonde actress were to climb out, exchange a few stormy words, then head for the waiting Maserati. Is that *all*? she thought. Child's play.

In take one the airboat overshot the jetty. In take two clouds of the blue smoke which belched from its engine drifted into the camera lens. In take three the actress stumbled. In take four someone sneezed. The airboat swooped back and forth across the water, its engine roaring at several hundred decibels. The temperature increased. Endlessly the action was stopped, started, repeated. There was an awful lot of waiting around. As the morning meandered on, Erin undertook a drastic reassessment. Her crack about 'reciting robots' had been patently untrue. Slipping into scripted emotion for a few seconds, only to be cut off in full spate, demanded a high degree of professionalism. The nervous strain had to be enormous. She noticed that while Jago and the actress lapsed into silent resignation at each break, Kiel was growing increasingly rattled. He paced around, demanding first a mirror, then a cold drink, then a cigarette, and all the time flaunting his irritation.

'The noise of that thing's giving me a sore head,' he complained, jerking a thumb at the airboat. 'And it's like a furnace inside this suit.'

Both actors were wearing suits; Kiel all in white, while Jago wore city-gent grey with a pearl-grey shirt. He looked very different from the man who sloped around in casual clothes and kicked off his shoes when he talked to her. But then, Erin recognised, he wasn't Jago Miles any more, he was a character in *Taro Beach*. His stance was different, his movements were different, even the angular planes of his face looked different. Reciting robot? Never.

'Can't we break for lunch?' grumbled Kiel, when the scene was repeated for the umpteenth time.

'Soon,' William promised. 'Let's give this one more try and please, go for realism, there's a good guy.'

Kiel did. The director was satisfied. Jago collected her and they ate a picnic lunch with the rest of the crew. Marvin and some of the others from the barbecue came over to talk, but it was noticeable that Kiel could only manage an offhand wave from the distance. And a merry Christmas to you too! she thought. Forty minutes later William began calling out for the second scene to be shot.

'Everything's as we rehearsed yesterday. To recap, you——' he pointed to the actress '— climb into the Maserati real quick to allow Jago and Kiel to slug it out. Kiel, you grab Jago. He throws you off, you grab again. You slam him right down across the bonnet and lean over. Allow a pause for him to catch his breath, then when he pushes back against your chest, you stagger. Just a step or two. Then the dialogue starts. Okay? And maintain the realism,' the director added.

Kiel scowled. 'You want realism, you got realism,' he muttered.

Everyone took their places. There was silence. A camera began to roll. A clapper-board clapped. As the actress disappeared inside the car, so the two men exchanged heated words. Next came a frozen tableau when they glared at each other. Viking versus Italian hit-man, Erin thought, unable to keep from comparing this confrontation with the one at the barbecue. Yet Jago wasn't versus anyone except her! The tableau sprang to life as Kiel gripped both lapels of his opponent's jacket. Instantly tanned hands chopped down to destroy his hold. He lunged again, spinning Jago around and off balance. Realism was one thing, but Kiel appeared to be using the scene as free licence to release his hostility for, with his fingers curled tight around Jago's shoulders, he viciously smashed him down. The Maserati was low slung, and Jago had a long backwards fall before he hit the bonnet. A thud rang out as his head cracked against the shiny silver metal. Erin winced. That must have hurt. For a moment Jago lay spreadeagled, then his hands were raised. Inches from making contact with the other man's chest, they fell. Kiel stepped backwards, and the entire film crew held its breath as their romantic lead slid slowly and unceremoniously to the ground.

'You stupid son of a bitch, Kiel!' cried William.

'It wasn't my fault,' he croaked, staring down in horror at the prostrate grey-suited form.

'Like hell it wasn't, you——' The director let rip with a string of highly coloured expletives. 'Bring some water,' he called, and everyone leapt to life.

In seconds Jago was surrounded by people on their knees, people flapping handkerchiefs, people standing up. Erin followed the swarm, but from the outer edge all she could see were occasional glimpses of him being propped up in a sitting position against the car. His arms hung limp. His eyes were open, but he did not seem to be focusing.

'Where's that water?' demanded William.

'Give him smelling salts,' somebody called.

'He's seeing stars.'

'He's fainted.'

'He's out for the count.'

The actress lifted his hand and patted it. A technician felt his brow.

'You fool, Kiel,' William blasted, and began a second berating. 'Why do you have to be so goddamn stupid? You know there's no time built into our schedule to allow for interruptions. All we've been allocated is this one day out here, and now you have to go and louse it up, you no-good, low-down——' Off went the expletives again.

'He's coming round,' said the actress, and

William ceased his curses mid-stream to bend over Jago and beam hopefully. Kiel used the diversion to slink away.

'All right, pal?' the director enquired. 'Better now? Let me give you a hand. We'll take it from the top again, but gently this time.'

Erin needed to stand on tiptoe to see what was happening. The director had slung Jago's arm around his shoulder and, with Marvin's help, was struggling to raise him. Given that he was six foot three and a dead weight, the task was not easy. When she saw how he was all slack arms and legs and vacant eyes, her Girl Guide training came back to her.

'You're not supposed to do that,' she called. 'You mustn't.' No one took any notice. 'Excuse me.' Erin began pushing forward. 'Excuse me, please.' Her request must have struck the correct note of importance, for now the people parted like the Red Sea and she ended up in the centre of the circle. 'Er, Jago'll be in shock,' she explained to William, somewhat surprised to find herself fronting the crowd. 'He shouldn't be moved. He needs to rest and—oh, he should be given a cup of hot, sweet tea.'

Marvin, his head buried beneath Jago's armpit, looked up, very impressed. 'Are you a doctor as well as a writer?' he enquired.

'Er, no.'

'You've been trained as a nurse?'

'Er, no.' Erin's cheeks flamed. All eyes were fastened expectantly upon her, and relating how she had been the leader of the Kingfisher Patrol some fifteen years previously did not seem much of a qualification. 'I have a little bit of medical know-how,' she proclaimed, trying her best to sound positive. Like anyone else, she did not relish making a fool of herself.

Jago guffawed. At least to her it sounded like a guffaw, though everyone else seemed to interpret it as a groan.

'All is not well,' he announced, in a tone which started out as ringing, but which dropped with a clang. 'I doubt some foul play.'

'Now, pal,' soothed William. 'I know Kiel was hasty, but you mustn't take this too hard.'

'I think he's quoting from *Hamlet*,' Erin intruded. 'When you're concussed you can sometimes say irrelevant things. You see, concussion's a bruising of part of the brain as the result of a blow.'

'You sure know your medicine,' praised Marvin. 'Come on, William, I guess we'd better take Erin's advice and let him rest.'

Jago was carefully lowered to the ground and propped up against the Maserati once more. There was a movement in the crowd, and someone miraculously produced a flask of tea.

'How many sugars do I give him?' William enquired.

'Four.' Even to herself Erin sounded efficient. 'And we need more space.'

'Space. Space.' Marvin took up the chant and began shooing off the onlookers as if they were troublesome pigeons. 'You heard what the lady said. Space.' People began to drift away.

'How long before he recovers?' William enquired, handing over the brimming cup.

'Hard to tell.' Jago had begun to blink, which she

took to be a sign of recovery. 'I'd say at least half an hour.'

'Okay folks, thirty minutes,' William hollered, and Marvin and the dregs of their audience ambled off to find some shade.

'It could be longer,' Erin protested. She tasted the tea to check it wasn't too hot, then knelt down. To her relief Jago sipped obediently.

'Thirty minutes maximum. *Taro Beach* is more or less an assembly line production and the machinery isn't geared to cope with delays,' the director informed her. 'In thirty minutes Jago'll be fine. Won't you, pal?'

'He might not be.'

Her patient gave an idiot's smile. 'Shall I compare thee to a summer's day?' he enquired.

William frowned. 'Say again?'

Jago moved his head and winced. He raised a slow hand to the back of his head, then brought it round to stare at his fingers. 'Blood,' he said dopily. He focused on her for a second. 'Erin, it hurts.'

'Oh, gee, don't let him get blood on his suit,' yelped the director. 'We're not carrying a spare.'

She threw him a filthy look. That Jago might be in pain came a long way down the scale. She disposed of the cup and made an examination. At the back of his head she found a patch of blond hair sticky with blood.

'The skin's broken. Jago ought to see a doctor,' she declared.

William sat back on his haunches. 'And where do you suggest we find a doctor, out here in the wilds? Nah.' He gave the bloody patch a quick look. 'It's not much. He'll be okay.'

'Okay,' slurred Jago.

'See, he's coming round,' William rejoiced. 'Take off his jacket, will you? Can't risk it getting stained. And how about his shirt?'

Erin rounded on him. 'Would you like me to take off his trousers, too?' she demanded, and Jago produced another guffaw. 'That cut should be cleaned. It may even require to be stitched.'

'Stitched!' Horror hit the director so hard he almost toppled over. 'We don't have time for stitches. Every minute our production overruns costs dollars, plenty dollars. And if Jago has stitches, then I guess they might need to shave off some of his hair. They mustn't do that'. He jumped to his feet. 'I'll fetch a cloth and some water. If you clean up the blood he'll be——'

'He needs to see a doctor,' she insisted, easing Jago's arms from his jacket.

'Sweetheart, you don't understand what's at stake here.' William dropped back and began to speak in a furtive whisper, his eyes circling to make sure no one was within earshot. 'This is a very fragile time for *Taro Beach.* We've slipped in the ratings, with our storylines I'm not surprised, and the whole shemozzle's in the melting pot. If the series folds our salaries will be sliced off——' he moved a hand '—— just like that. I finalised on a waterfront condominium just a few months back, and I'm in debt up to the hilt. Now is not the time for delays in production, any extra expenses. The accountancy boys insist we run on a shoestring. You've no idea the way I had to fight for the shoot in New York. I——'

'If Jago doesn't get to see a doctor, he may not be

fit enough to travel to New York,' she said, the words sizzling out of her like steam.

'Oh hell.' The director frowned. 'The blood's not running on to his shirt collar, is it?'

'No!'

Jago blinked, stretching his eyes open wide. 'I won't let you down, William,' he murmured. 'Give me a hand.'

'Don't you dare,' Erin threatened. 'Look at him. He's giddy. There's no way he can stand, and as for acting—forget it!'

'I think that shirt should come off,' William fretted.

Her teeth scraped together. 'You,' she said through them, 'have your priorities all wrong. Jago is concussed, his head is bleeding and he requires proper medical attention.'

'But what about *Taro Beach*?' came the wail.

'*Taro Beach* is something on celluloid, that's all. Where's the nearest hospital?'

'I don't know. I'm a stranger on this coast, like everyone else.'

Erin frowned. 'I think I know where there's one,' she said hesitantly, remembering that Maria had mentioned a hospital on the road which forked inland.

'Is it far?'

'Around fifteen, twenty miles—I think.'

William surveyed his romantic lead's helplessness, the pallor of his complexion.

'I guess you'd better take him. He's not going to be any use like this and I can't risk the New York shoot being loused up. Ask the doctors to dose him with painkillers or something, but whatever happens don't let them shave off his hair. And honey——' he gave a pleading smile, 'try not to let him get blood all over himself.'

The make-up girl provided a wad of paper tissues, and armed with these Erin clambered into the limousine. William and Marvin manoeuvred Jago in beside her and, with the rest of the unit watching from a respectful distance, they drove away. At the first bend her patient slumped against her, murmuring incoherently, and keeping him steady and trying to protect his wound became a full-time job.

'How far now?' asked the driver, when they arrived at the fork in the road.

'No idea. I know there's a hospital down here, but I don't know where. We'll just have to keep watch.'

Jago stirred. 'Don't want to go to hospital.'

'That cut must be looked at,' she said gently.

'No, it's fine.' With a determined effort, he pushed himself up to gaze blearily out at their surroundings. They were driving through grassland which spread for miles. 'Turn round,' he ordered the driver.

'Take no notice,' Erin countermanded. Something else she remembered from her Girl Guide days was that concussion could cause belligerence, and the scowl on Jago's face indicated he was running true to form. 'Do you have a headache?' she queried.

'A bit. No, I don't. I feel better now. I'm okay. I *am*. Let's just go back to the unit. Let's just——'

She ignored him and advised the driver to do the same. Jago muttered beneath his breath for a minute or two then sank into a sullen silence. Erin looked anxiously around. Fields, farms, wide open spaces were the order of the day. Had she misunderstood Maria? Then she saw a cluster of red brick buildings ahead and her spirits lifted.

'Here we are,' she announced, as they passed a 'Hospital' sign.

The driver grinned at her through the mirror, obviously as relieved as she was. He turned the car on to a drive which led through well-tended lawns to a porticoed entrance.

'I'll stay with Jago while you get things organised,' he suggested, when they came to a halt.

Erin walked into a low-ceilinged foyer. Carpeted in terracotta and filled with leafy green plants, the atmosphere was tranquil. She approached a reception desk and began to explain the situation to a nurse in crisp white. In response the emergency unit were contacted.

'Mr Miles will be attended to in a moment,' the nurse told her, then added conversationally, 'It's quite a change for us to be dealing with him as a patient when he's been our star visitor for so long. I don't think he's missed one Wednesday for over two years, and he comes most Sundays. He deserves a medal for devoted service. He—oh, excuse me.'

Two medics had arrived with a stretcher, and the nurse darted out to lead them to the portico. Jago was helped from the car, his wound subjected to a swift inspection and then, muttering protests, he was laid on the stretcher and wheeled away.

'Mild concussion,' the nurse confirmed, as she and Erin returned to the reception desk. 'The cut isn't deep, so I imagine Emergency'll just bathe it in antiseptic. He shouldn't be gone long. I suppose you'd like to trot along to Room 28 while you're waiting? His young lady's always ready to chat.'

'Er——'

Everything was happening too quickly. First Jago's Wednesday rendezvous had been revealed, now she was being offered more. She needed time to think. Did she say yes? Did she say no? Erin was faced with a dilemma. She was reluctant to intrude on what was glaringly an area he wanted kept secret, and yet . . . Didn't she have her profile to consider? The nurse took her silence as acquiesence and dialled a number.

'What name do I say?' she enquired.

A lip was nibbled, then, 'Erin Page.'

CHAPTER SIX

MEMORISING instructions, she set off down a wide corridor. Was she on the brink of discovering that elusive piece of jigsaw which, when fitted in, would reveal the full and clear picture of Jago's life? It seemed so. And a full and clear picture meant she could write a full and clear profile. A profile of merit. Delight added a spring to her step. Yet as she walked along delight began to waver, and in its place came apprehension. Her step slowed.

'His young lady's longing to see you,' the nurse had reported.

Erin fiddled with the strap of her shoulder bag. The person on the other end of the phone had known about her, but it was one-way traffic. She felt uncomfortable, at a disadvantage. Who waited in Room 28? The name which sprang to mind had to be Olivia's because, thinking back, she realised Jago had never said the actress was dead. Erin scolded herself for jumping to conclusions, both then and now. His young lady could be anyone. But why was she in hospital?

As Erin veered to allow free passage to a porter pushing a trolley, an agony of indecision gripped. No need to be told Room 28 and its occupant were off-limits, so should she turn right around and head back to reception? Was that the decent thing to do? She felt a pang of unease, and stood immobile for a long minute. But it wasn't as though she had made enquiries, turned over stones, poked her nose in. Fate was responsible for bringing her here, and who was she to quarrel with fate? Jago couldn't blame her for taking an opportunity which had been dumped in her lap.

Erin frowned, starting to walk again. Yes, he could. And he would. Verbal pyrotechnics would burst around her head when he learnt she had solved the puzzle of the mysterious Wednesdays. But on reflection he must agree her profile provided a legitimate excuse—mustn't he? He would understand how she needed to know the truth, to write the truth, for all the proper reasons—wouldn't he?

She passed surgical wards and a physiotherapy unit, patients in dressing gowns, hurrying nurses, and eventually reached a door marked 28. Squaring her shoulders, Erin knocked. Think positive, think profile, she told herself.

'Come in,' called a voice, and she entered a room filled with sunshine.

Decorated in corn-gold and white, with a yellow carpet, floral curtains which lifted on the breeze, a television set and video, the room was luxuriously equipped. Sprays of fresh blossoms added a fragrance, and there were baskets of fruit. Beside the window sat a girl—in a wheelchair.

Erin's thoughts took off in a breathtaking spiral. Blonde and in her early twenties, this was not Olivia.

'Hi, I'm Susie. I've been dying to meet you,' she grinned, steering forward and holding out a slender hand.

Trying to mask her confusion, Erin murmured a

greeting. She well remembered Jago's mention of Susie, but who was she?

'For the past three weeks Jago's conversation has been peppered with references to a knock-out intellectual who's flown over from England,' the girl said, with a teasing lilt. 'And I was eager to see whether or not you do have two heads. Not that I ever imagined I would. Family and friends pass through Jago's security screen, no problem, but anyone with the faintest whiff of the media is kept well away. Take a bow. You're the first writer to receive my brother's top level clearance.'

Brother? Instantly Erin saw the resemblance. The girl was a slight, feminine version of Jago, though without the skew-whiff nose. The diaries had named the youngest of his sisters as Suzanne, a sibling he affectionately called 'the kid'. His comments about this baby of the family had been sparse, and now she began to understand why. He must have been wary of her making a connection with the girl he had demanded news about at the poolside.

'I haven't had top level clearance or any clearance,' Erin confessed. 'The only reason I'm here is because the nurse——'

'Poll?'

'No. Does Poll work at this hospital?' she asked, realising as she spoke that she would. 'We've never met. I've only seen her from a distance.'

'Poll's my night-time angel.' Susie's fine brows dipped. 'But if Jago didn't give permission and Poll isn't involved, how come you're here at all?'

Taking care to emphasise her brother's injury was slight, Erin explained. 'A few minutes ago he was whisked off to Emergency. The nurse in reception presumed I was a friend and suggested I might like to see you.'

There was a giggle. 'So when Jago calls in to visit me and discovers you've arrived first, he's liable to flip his lid?'

'I don't think he will call in. He's in a rush to return to the set. Every minute counts.'

Susie made a moue of protest. 'But he flies off to New York tomorrow. I know he's already said his goodbyes and that he'll telephone every day, but even so——' Her face brightened. 'Say, how about you and me hightailing it down to the emergency unit and giving him one big surprise?'

'If you want to go and surprise him, please do. I'd rather not.' Erin's smile was tepid. 'As you said, he could well flip his lid when he discovers his security screen has been breached.'

'But Jago in the full flight of fury is always worth watching,' his sister proclaimed, laughing.

'Not when the fury's directed straight here.' Erin flattened a hand on her chest. 'He already has a sore head. Is it fair to make it worse?'

'I take your point. Okay, we'll leave him be.'

'Thanks.'

'I could suffer a bout of amnesia where you're concerned,' Susie offered. 'But on one condition, that you visit me while Jago's in New York.' She smiled appealingly. 'I understand he's been talking to you about his childhood. Maybe I could add to that?'

'Done,' Erin agreed promptly. Visiting Susie would make a refreshing break to her routine, and if she could add another source of information to her profile, that was a bonus. She inspected her watch. 'Another couple of minutes then it's vital I get back to reception. I'd hate your brother to miss me and launch a full-scale search.'

'Coward!' Susie gestured towards a bedside photograph which showed a smiling, dark-haired young man. 'On your next visit I'll introduce you to Robert. He's also been wondering what an Oxford graduate looks like.' She gazed adoringly at the picture. 'Robert's my boyfriend. He's paraplegic, like me. He shattered his spine falling from a horse, my accident was in a car.' She tilted her head, the blonde hair dropping down in a straight line. 'Or did you know that?'

'I—I guessed,' Erin admitted. 'Have you been here ever since?'

'No, the first six months were spent in Thailand, that's where the crash happened. Initially it was too dangerous for me to be moved, but when I grew stronger Jago chartered a plane and brought me here.'

'Why here?'

'Because he'd made enquiries and discovered that the resident surgeon, Dr Heger, is one of the finest where spinal reclamation is concerned.' Susie laughed. 'Though he charges the earth. Jago hoped I might be able to be patched up as good as new, but it's not to be. I've had a series of operations, the last was just three weeks ago.'

'On the Saturday?' Erin asked.

'That's right. How did you know?'

'I first met Jago on the Sunday morning. He was—wound up. Then when I saw him later in the day his tension had eased.'

'It figures. He came along mid-morning to check I was okay. I was. He gets far more worked up over these things than I do. Jago gives all the appearance of being laid back, but he isn't. He worries about me, and my brothers and sisters. He's saddled with a highly developed sense of responsibility. Too highly developed, Robert says. Mind you, with parents like ours it's a good thing someone was around to take charge. Oops,' her hand clamped over her mouth. 'I shouldn't have said that. Big brother objects when I criticise. His motto is "United we stand, etc."' Susie gulped in an excited breath. 'But the last operation was the final one, and now I want to be united with Robert. We're making wedding plans. In two months' time we're both due to be discharged, then——' Erin received a slightly defensive glance. 'We can manage fine, we know we can. Robert's career is in computers, so him being in a wheelchair's no problem. All we need is a house constructed to meet our require-ments, plus a car each,' she added, with a toss of her fingers, 'then we'll be independent. I admit a house would be a major expense, but once we were installed Jago won't need to spend another bean. Robert insists that when we're Mr and Mrs we support ourselves. Mrs Robert Pierce,' she crooned. 'Sounds great, doesn't it?'

'Great. Jago would provide the house and the cars?'

'My brother's the most generous guy imaginable,' Susie announced gaily. 'I've done my sums and I figure a custom-built property in a prime position would cost around six months of his *Taro Beach* salary. Robert maintains we could do it much cheaper, but why should we? Jago likes me to have the best.' Her brow creased in a moment of irritation. 'Trouble is, he's holding back on us getting married and I can't understand why. He swears he likes Robert, but I have my doubts. Why else would he insist we're rushing things when we're not? I asked Jago to come with us to look over some land which was for sale, but he made excuses.' A strand of flaxen hair was twisted around a finger. 'I don't think he's convinced that Robert and me should set up home together.'

'Perhaps—well, perhaps—well, you did say a house would be a major expense,' Erin faltered. It was not her place to reveal Jago's *Taro Beach* salary might not be as automatic as Susie believed, but didn't she deserve a hint?

'Money isn't the issue. Jago has plenty.'

'Yes?' She frowned, then, remembering the time, leapt to her feet. 'I must go.' She made her farewells. 'When shall I come again?'

'Tomorrow,' Susie said decisively.

'Tomorrow it is.'

Several people were sitting around the foyer, but none of them was Jago. When Erin made enquiries at the reception desk the nurse, a different woman from the one she had spoken with earlier, made a noise of exasperation.

'You've missed him by minutes. You must be the young lady he was looking for.'

'What was the verdict on his head?' she asked anxiously.

'All clear, no stitches were needed. Emergency cleaned him up, handed over a couple of aspirin and sent him on his way.' The nurse smiled at her relief, then continued, 'We searched everywhere for you, but Mr Miles had to leave. Something about production time overrunning. He said to give you his apologies and ask if you'll follow him on. Shall I fix a cab?'

'If you would.'

'Where do you want to go?' the nurse enquired, lifting the receiver.

Erin looked blank. All she knew was that they had turned off the main road on to a track and driven for a good ten minutes before reaching the *Taro Beach* unit. The track had been one of several, all unmarked, and the Everglades had a sameness about it.

She sighed. 'To the Driftwood Motel, please.'

Before arriving at Jago's home that evening, much serious thought took place. Erin obliterated any doubts about whether she had acted correctly in going to see Susie, and instead fell back on the conviction that fate's hand had pointed the way. Fate had also arranged for her to be heading back there tomorrow, plus fate had ensured Jago was disappearing for a whole week. Everything had been preordained with a view to her compiling the finest and most complete profile possible.

Standing on his doorstep, she adjusted her grip on her briefcase. Now she knew the direction the profile would take—given Jago's agreement. His agreement was the crunch. At present a gap existed between what she wanted to write and what she knew he would allow, but couldn't that gap be bridged? If she chose exactly the right moment, exactly the right mood, and if her argument was persuasive enough, Jago must agree. She had no doubt fate would lend a helping hand there, too. Refusing to fret about the mechanics of gaining permission, Erin rang the doorbell. First she must listen to what Susie had to say. Second she must assemble facts pertinent to a responsible and sensitive profile. Third that profile must be drafted, and then . . .

'How are you feeling?' she enquired, when Jago greeted her. She searched his face, but the pallor had gone. He looked fit and alert, and very pleased to see her.

'The cut's sore, but my head doesn't ache any more.'

'No after-effects?'

'None,' he assured her.

Erin hovered uncertainly. 'I rang earlier to ask if you felt up to talking, but your answering machine replied. Even though you're feeling okay, I quite understand if you want an early night.'

'You think I'm crazy enough to turn away my very own Florence Nightingale?' The crinkle-eyed smile dazzled. 'But what would I do if I suffer a relapse and need you to cool my fevered brow?'

He took hold of her elbow to usher her into the house. The aloofness of the past couple of days had disappeared, it was obvious they were friends once more. Erin's first reaction was relief, but was relief appropriate? Instead of giving three cheers perhaps she should run for cover? Jago's appeal was considerable, and already the touch of his hand on her arm had speeded up her blood.

'You couldn't reach me earlier because I've only been home ten minutes,' he explained, as they sat down in the living-room. 'William was determined to complete the day's schedule if it killed him.'

'Or if it killed you!'

'He isn't your favourite man?'

'No way. I was under the impression directors possessed the understanding of Freud and the philosophical flair of Socrates, but William!' She let out a breath. 'All he cares about is *Taro Beach*. Talk about single-minded!'

'Aren't other people equally single-minded?' Jago enquired, his tone lazy, his eyes not. 'About stone, about writing books? You looked after me today and I have a whole list of thanks prepared,' he continued, speeding up. 'Before I start on them though, I must apologise for leaving you stranded at the hospital. When I couldn't make contact there seemed no alternative but to return to the unit.' He lifted his hips to slide his hands into his trouser pockets. 'Where were you?' he enquired.

'Out walking.' Erin found a thread of lint on her scarlet jeans. 'I arrived back at reception just minutes after you'd gone, but I couldn't follow because I didn't know the way. I took a taxi to the motel instead.'

'So that's what happened. When you didn't appear I presumed you'd got bored.' A grin curved his mouth. 'I'm well aware filming can come over as the most tedious activity ever known to man.'

'It was interesting,' she defended, then, as his grin spread, amended, 'and tedious.' She paused in unfastening her briefcase. 'If you came back just ten minutes ago you won't have had dinner?'

'I don't feel like eating.'

'You must! After what's happened today you

need food. If not you might start feeling faint.'

Jago stretched back in the chair, his hands still in his pockets. With his long legs spread, the material was pulled tight across his thighs. Must he lie there looking so—male? Erin wondered, suddenly stricken by his attractiveness, his virility.

'But if I faint you'll need to give me the kiss of life. Your mouth over mine can't be bad. Okay, okay.' The blue eyes were wide with innocent repentance. 'I'll eat something later.'

'You'll eat something now.' Unable to stay still and look at him any longer, Erin surged into action. 'Let's go and see what Maria's provided. And if you don't fancy it, maybe I can rustle up something to your liking?'

'Yeah, boss,' Jago drawled, and laughed when she wrinkled her nose in reply. 'From what I hear you were also giving your orders earlier today,' he teased, following her into the kitchen. 'I have a vague recollection of you taking charge, but when I returned to the set Marvin rushed to give chapter and verse. That guy's a fully paid-up member of your fan club. He's also under the impression you dabble in brain surgery in your spare time.' His amused tone faded. 'I gather there wasn't too much milk of human kindness being splashed around until you took charge. I want to thank you for your concern.'

'My pleasure,' she replied, trying to keep things casual. Did he know that when he smiled at her like that she was tempted to move close, to touch him, to . . . Erin held out a plate she had taken from the fridge. 'Cold meat salad?' Jago's response was a shudder, so she ran her eyes over the shelves. 'How about hamburgers, or gammon and eggs, or omelette, or——'

'Omelette, with some of this.' He pointed to a slab of cheese. 'If it's not too much trouble.'

'Trouble? You're looking at a girl who makes omelettes while she pats her stomach *and* rubs her head.' To prove her point, she became hyperactive. The pan was heating on the stove, the eggs were whisked, a place was set at the pine table in minutes. 'Coffee or tea, sir?'

'Coffee, please.' Jago sat with his elbows on the table, his chin in his hands, watching as she waltzed around. 'I like you,' he murmured. 'Am I allowed to like or does that contravene the biographer's rules?'

'Liking's permissible.' Erin found that grating cheese required intense concentration. 'I trust Kiel went easy when it came to smashing you down on the Maserati a second time around?'

'He did, plus the third, fourth and fifth time.' He saw her dismay. 'Don't panic, he was gentleness itself. How dare he be anything else with William muttering threats from the sidelines?' A wry brow tweaked. 'I understand your education has been enhanced by some choice obscenities?'

Nodding, Erin slid the omelette on to a warm plate. 'My education has also been enhanced by the knowledge that *Taro Beach* could well be destined for the chop.'

'William told you?' Jago sighed. 'Okay, so I reckoned the drop in ratings was a hiccup, but the litany of show business is don't talk failure, and bad news travels like wildfire.'

'You think I'd have rushed out and shouted your confidences from the rooftops?' she rebuked.

'No, I don't but—well, I guess I have a habit of keeping things close to my chest.'

'Is there life for you after *Taro Beach*?' she enquired, setting the plate before him.

'I don't know.' Jago began to eat. There was a long stretch of time before he spoke again. 'To be honest I can't imagine anyone rushing to sign up an actor so closely identified with a soap opera, especially a failed soap opera,' he admitted. He ate on for a while, before continuing, 'For years I've itched to try my hand at directing. Once I did start to save up with the idea of financing a film of my own, just a low-budget production, but the cash wasn't there. This would have been the ideal time to have had a go. Directing would have removed me from the screen, allowed the character I play a chance to fade from the public's memory, but——' He shrugged and threw a quick glance across the table. 'You must wonder what I do with my money. This is off the record, but a couple of years back one of my sisters had a long spell in hospital abroad. At first she was in intensive care, then round-the-clock attention was required, specialist nursing, expensive drugs. In order to pay the bills I begged and borrowed all over the place, and as a result landed myself on a financial treadmill. When I joined *Taro Beach* I had a huge backlog of debts to settle, plus current outgoings, plus future demands on my earnings.' He threw her another quick glance. 'I'm not complaining. If families can't provide support when it's needed, we might as well give up. I also recognise I'm extremely fortunate to have earned the sums I have. All I'm saying is that I'm not as stinking rich as it would appear. There's invariably an account to meet, a forthcoming expense to be borne in mind. Stop it, Erin,' he ordered suddenly.

'Stop what?'

'Stop thinking about all this in terms of your goddamn profile.'

'I'm not.'

'You are. I can recognise that crusading gleam in your eye. I don't think there's ever twenty consecutive minutes go by without you thinking about your profile.' He jammed his lips together. 'You know it's scary the way you evaluate everything with your writing in mind, but if you think there's a chance of portraying Jago Miles as a good Samaritan in the gospel according to Erin Page, you can think again.'

She opened her mouth, then closed it again unable to meet his attack. She *had* been thinking about the profile, but why not? And it wasn't a case of portraying him as a good Samaritan, it was a case of portraying Jago as Jago. His generosity was an integral part of the man.

'Money apart, won't you be relieved to be free of *Taro Beach*?' she enquired hesitantly.

She received a baleful glance.

'I knew you'd get around to that. You never did believe it was a good career move, did you? This is off the record again, but yes. I badly want to return to acting and not re-acting.'

'You *do* act in *Taro Beach*,' Erin protested.

'Thanks.' He grinned, easier now. 'Yes, I try to get inside my character, but the whole series is so over the top it's unbelievable. Given the chance I'd like to do something multi-faceted, something that stretches, makes me take risks.' Jago pushed aside the empty plate. 'What the hell. I'll survive whether I act or not. I can always dig ditches. And if your writing ever palls, you can always find work as a cook.' He beamed. 'That omelette was delicious.'

'Glad you approved.'

There was a timeless moment when they sat and smiled at each other, then Erin reached to begin clearing away.

'Don't.' His hand covered hers. 'Maria can do that tomorrow.' He ran a finger across the back of her wrist. 'You know what I'd like to happen now, toots?' he enquired softly. 'I'd like us to take our coffee through to the living-room, me to have a cigar, us both to sip brandies. Then I could talk into that machine of yours for a while—just to keep you happy—and later I'd like us to wander upstairs and make slow, easy love. It's been a long time since I've had a woman in my bed and I suspect it's an even longer time since you've had a man in yours.' Jago frowned. 'No, I'm saying this badly. I don't want a woman, I want you. And I think you want me. I want to hold you near and kiss you, and——'

'Jago.'

'I wouldn't start exclaiming in that horrified tone of yours if I were you,' he murmured, his finger moving back and forth across the bones of her hand. 'You know how amorous it makes me. But I reckon you should have got the hang of me by now. Have I rushed off nights to rape and pillage? Has a stream of women flitted around my house in a state of undress? Aren't I impressing you with my sobriety?'

She gazed at him, her brown eyes wide and troubled. 'Yes, but——'

'I'm not asking you for a one night stand, just a quick roll in the hay. In fact I'm not quite sure what I'm asking for at all—but, as Burt would say, trust me. I think you need me and I know damn well I need you. Don't you ever yearn to feel arms around you in the middle of the night, to know the wonderful release of——'

'I can't.' Erin swallowed. 'It's not that I don't like you because I do, but——'

'I'm not talking about *liking*, dammit! I'm talking about——' He broke off to glower, snatching his fingers from hers. 'What the hell does it matter what I'm talking about? Us coming together is against your professional ethics, that's why you're getting so damned uptight *again*.' His voice had gathered an icy edge. 'Tell me, is there a time scale on this? Are we allowed to fraternise once the book's published or must I wait ten years before the 'hands off' clause expires? And where will I find you in ten years' time, still stuck in your cottage with your cat, writing, writing, writing? There has to be more to life than putting words on paper.' Jago caught hold of her hand again. 'Doesn't there?'

'Yes.' The word emerged as a whisper.

'Time's passing by, Erin, and who knows what tomorrow might bring?' A cloud crossed his eyes. He was thinking of Susie, she knew he was. 'You're young, healthy, intelligent. You should be making commitments to something more than a damned manuscript!'

'Yes.' This time the word sounded stronger. Her spine straightened. 'Okay, we'll take our coffees through, have a brandy, go upstairs——'

'And?' he asked, when she hesitated.

'And I'll wash your hair. There's a stiff patch at the back where the blood was cleaned off. Jago Miles can't take New York by storm unless he's looking his best.'

'No?' His laugh was faint and dry. 'Maybe you're right.'

Coffee and brandies were drunk. Jago talked about one of the Ibsen productions he had appeared in, and time passed. It was nearly eleven o'clock by the time they reached the bathroom. A spray fitment was attached to the bath, and he stripped off his shirt and dropped down beside it.

'Be gentle with me?' he begged, grinning up.

Erin made a careful inspection. 'It's amazing how such a tiny cut produced so much blood.'

'Shows how macho I am, all that rich red stuff pouring out.'

She wetted his hair. 'You don't look macho to me, kneeling down like that with your eyes tight shut. You look like a little boy. Maybe a big little boy,' she amended, starting to lather. 'Am I hurting?'

'No.'

'Don't shake your head, dumbo, otherwise I might.' The shampoo was rinsed off, then she repeated the process and rinsed again. 'Rise, Sir Jago,' she grinned, blotting his head with a towel.

While he had been below her everything had been under control, but as he stood the perspective underwent a dramatic change. Erin was conscious of the bareness of his chest, the gleaming tanned skin, his muscular shoulders. Her heartbeat quickened. A droplet of water slid down his jaw, and she reached to dab it away. The moment she touched him, she knew her mistake. An emotion flickered in his eyes, only to be matched by an echoing flicker inside her. With his hair damp and tousled, he was a long way from the smooth Mr Wonderful of *Taro Beach*, yet he seemed infinitely more desirable. Erin's skin itched, her mouth went dry. There was an impatient yearning, a need. If he asked her now to make love, she would agree. Whatever he commanded, she would obey. She forgot about the profile, she forgot about the lessons Ned had taught her. If tomorrow she had to pay, so be it, but for tonight . . .

'Enough,' Jago said harshly. He clasped her head in both his hands and drew her to him. He kissed her roughly once, twice, and then took a deep shuddering breath. 'You must go.'

'Must I?'

'Mustn't you?'

The air throbbed.

'Yes.' Common sense had made a comeback. She had been leading with her heart and not her head, but in that direction lay disaster. 'I'll keep my fingers crossed that the New York shoot goes well and that *Taro Beach* takes an upturn.'

Jago didn't hear. He had folded his arms and was studying her. 'I don't understand you,' he frowned.

'I don't understand myself.' Erin gave a tremulous smile. 'I hope you avoid being mauled by the fans.'

'I will, if I follow your example.'

'What—what does that mean? she asked, aware

that the blueness of his gaze had backed her into a corner, a cold corner.

'It means that if I keep my head down and devote myself entirely to my work, I'm bound to emerge unscathed.'

CHAPTER SEVEN

In response to Susie's pleas her hospital visit the next day was repeated the subsequent afternoon and the following one, to become a regular event right through until the day of Jago's return. She and Susie hit it off well. The girl in the wheelchair was an appealing personality—candid, a touch spoilt perhaps, but with a bubbly spirit. Robert, who turned out to be far more pragmatic and down to earth, made the perfect partner. Holding hands as they chatted, the young couple were very much in love. They were also very keen to plan the future which, in Susie's view, hinged on being lavished with a dream house. Yet when she disappeared, wheeling off to round up soft drinks, Robert's ambivalence towards outside help became clear. He told Erin that if Jago wanted to finance a property he would be grateful, but . . .

Susie's account of the Miles family childhood made an interesting contrast to her brother's. Shared situations took on a completely new slant, reminding Erin, yet again, how the same facts can fall into different patterns when viewed from different standpoints, yet be equally valid. Whereas Jago seemed to subscribe to the theory that if you're stuck in a situation you can't change, you get on and cope, the family's baby had been content for others to cope for her. 'Others' had often meant her eldest brother. Over the days there were references to Jago bandaging scraped knees, taking her to school, even jogging Ursula's memory when a new party dress was required.

'Jago is brother, protector, friend, father—all rolled into one,' Susie affirmed fondly, 'and not just with me. You should see him in action here.' She grinned at Erin's furrowed brow. 'His Wednesdays were originally set aside to keep me from becoming lonesome,' she explained. 'Friends and family visit as often as they can—Jago's always happy to shell out for air tickets, gasoline, you name it—but when I first arrived I went through a very blue period when I was desperate not to be left alone. In time that passed. I made friends, didn't need so much support, and Jago started to take an interest in what else was happening around the spinal injuries unit. Now he goes into the gym, helps out at hydrotherapy sessions. Everyone's amazed to meet a TV star who comes across as normal.'

'He *is* normal,' Erin protested, then blushed at the fervour of her defence. 'If only I could put this into the profile,' she remarked wistfully, 'but he wouldn't agree.'

'No. His version is he's not helping anyone, they're helping him by being an antidote to the artificial world of show business.' Susie shrugged. 'The kids in particular think Jago's great, but he's always had a knack with kids. He was marvellous with me when I was young.' A strand of pale hair was picked from a shoulder. 'I've often wondered why our parents bothered to produce one child, let alone half a dozen. On the face of it you'd think six blocks of granite would have suited Ursula better.

Still, even if she was haphazard, she did love us. Olivia's mother didn't love her.' There was a pause. 'Has Jago ever mentioned Olivia?'

'Only to say she's a closed chapter.'

'She is.' Susie's mouth pinched up. 'The one positive aspect of the crash was that it removed her—and good riddance!'

Erin gulped. 'You mean she's—she's dead?' she questioned, as the harsh verdict revived her earlier surmisings.

'Heavens, no.' Hoots of derision filled the room. 'Olivia's like a cat, always lands on her feet. The last I heard she'd fastened her claws into some L.A. film mogul. Once again she'll be poised to leap into the big time. It's incredible how skilled she can be at persuading people to open doors, then achieving sweet nothing once she's inside.' Susie was sneering. 'Jago opened doors. He should have had more sense.'

'But he tried to help her because he loved her,' Erin said, using the voice of reason.

'Just shows how blind love can be! Olivia had already spent six, seven years getting nowhere when she met him, and even to an outsider like me it was plain she didn't have what it takes,' Susie continued, using the same sneering tone. 'But Jago made a point of introducing her to the right people, directing her towards openings, and then bore the brunt of her frustration when her career lay flat as a pancake. She could be real vindictive at times, but he took it all. The dummy! I know there must have been good moments for them—why else would Jago have been so attentive?—but from my angle it seemed an odd affair. And it was me who

introduced them!' She heaved a sigh of regret.
'Olivia was a friend of a friend of mine, and because
she dropped such heavy hints I arranged for her to
meet Jago. She can be vivacious, good company
when she wants to be, and he was attracted. Only
attracted,' the girl in the wheelchair stressed.
'Funny thing is, it wasn't as though she'd hit him
like ten thousand volts, which makes no sense of
why they stuck together. I'd have said much of the
initial attraction was that, like any man, Jago found
it difficult to resist someone who gave such a
splendid performance of being besotted.'

'It was only a performance?'

'No,' came the grudging admission. 'I think she
genuinely did fall for him, but there were many
other threads to what she felt. There's no doubt she
derived a kick from being seen around with a well-
known actor, someone who had status, though as
the months went by there was a backlash.' Susie
turned down her mouth. 'Olivia began to resent
Jago being the one always fussed over. When she
voiced her complaints, he did his best to compen-
sate. He tried to keep an even lower profile than
usual, and pushed her forward instead. From the
start of their relationship Olivia had followed Jago
to wherever his work took him, and now she
declared she'd sacrificed her career for his. Who
was she kidding! If she'd been offered a job he
wouldn't have seen her heels for the dust.' Susie
dripped scorn. 'I told him at the time he was being
taken advantage of, but he came down on me like a
ton of bricks. Reckoned I didn't understand.'

'Greater love hath no man than this,' Erin quoted
ruefully and not altogether appropriately.

'Huh! I even approached Olivia privately and appealed for her to quit hustling him, but all she did was dissolve into tears and play "poor little me". She was a whiz when it came to pathos. She said why did I resent my brother giving her chances when so far she'd had such a raw deal out of life? Wasn't she entitled to her share of good fortune? What was wrong with reaching from the gutter for the stars? As a kid she'd had a squalid time, and she used that to great effect.'

Erin was intrigued. 'What had happened to her?'

'It was the classic case of a drunk for a father and a couldn't-care-less mother. Whereas Ursula carted the six of us around everywhere, Olivia's mom couldn't wait to be rid of her. The kid was dumped anyplace while her mother headed for the nearest bar or dance hall. As Olivia told it, she was always in the way, always neglected. She grew up grabbing love and attention wherever she could.' Susie became pensive. 'She had a great big streak of vulnerability, and I guess Jago, soft-hearted mutt that he is, responded to it. He'd have been far better off if he'd cut loose, but he was always so *concerned* about her.'

'So how did the car crash remove Olivia?'

Silence. A taut silence. Susie frowned, rubbing a finger on the arm of her wheelchair. 'I don't——'

'Forgive me, I'm being insensitive,' Erin said quickly, scolding herself for asking the question. She should have realised such memories would be everlastingly painful. If Susie spoke about the crash she must do so of her own accord, and not be prodded. 'Remember your amnesia where my visits are concerned?' she queried, hurdling her mistake.

'I've kept quiet when Jago's phoned through from New York,' Susie assured her.

'Thanks, but come Sunday the amnesia can end. All this week I've been working on a draft of my profile and although it's open-ended because I've still to hear more about Jago's career, it is taking shape. On Saturday I plan to plonk it down before him and with luck avert an explosion. You did agree I could mention you so I have, sparingly, and——'

'I don't understand how you hope to avert an explosion,' Susie interrupted. 'When Jago reads my name and realises we've met, my guess is he'll embark on a full flight of fury.'

Erin shook her head, the brown curls tumbling. 'There's no mawky sentiment, no purple prose, no drum beating. In fact there's nothing at all in the profile to which Jago can take exception.'

Susie grinned. 'You hope.'

'I *know.*'

The determination to compress as much as possible into the period of Jago's absence meant that at first she had collected up her notes and typewriter at the end of each day, and staggered back to the motel for a further session. Then Maria had made a suggestion.

'Why not work on at the house, hon? That way you won't disturb anyone with the rattle of keys. I'm sure our lord and master won't mind.' The housekeeper had smiled. 'And I can make you a bit to eat to stop you from fading away.'

Erin had given thanks and settled down in the pink and white bedroom where she was free to type, play back tapes, study notes to her heart's content.

Each evening she had worked through until ten, when tools had been downed and she had summoned a cab. Even she had her limits.

As Wednesday presented the last opportunity for following this régime, she was eager to make the most of it. She said goodbye to Maria and the girls, ate the pizza provided, and returned to her labours. Jago had called the previous day to ask how she was getting along and had mentioned that he was booked on to a late flight. He would not be home until midnight, but by then she would be long gone.

Reading through the paragraph she had just typed, Erin smiled. Everything was flowing. Although this was only a first draft and incomplete, she knew it was a good draft. A good draft augured well for a good book, a very good book, a wonderful book. With a contented sigh, she turned back to the typewriter. Her fingers were raised to the keys when suddenly she frowned. Erin tilted her head. Was that a noise downstairs? She strained to listen. Yes, there were noises. For a moment she went cold, fearing intruders, then she relaxed. A key had been turned in a lock, then came the sound of the front door being opened and closed. No intruders, this would be Jago home early.

Jago! Into action she dived, ripping the paper from her machine, bundling up her draft and pushing it into a folder. The folder was shoved inside her briefcase, and the briefcase fastened. Timing was everything. And timing meant it was vital he didn't know about her draft until Saturday. She dare not risk him idly lifting a page and reading his sister's name ahead of time. If she was to gain agreement to Susie's inclusion, then her hand must be on the tiller, things must be steered her way. Rapidly she set a pile of press cuttings to one side of the desk and inserted a clean sheet in the typewriter.

She scanned her work base. Yes, all tracks had been covered. No one would ever guess she was currently involved in something which might be termed 'clandestine'.

Tucking her mocha silk shirt more neatly into the waistband of her slacks, Erin set off down the landing to greet him. At the top of the stairs, a welling of emotion halted her. Jago was below in the hall, his back towards her. Head bent, slightly stooped, he was in the process of patting his pockets, perhaps in search of cigars. Her eyes moved over him; lingering on the thick fair hair which curled at the nape of his neck, on the width of his shoulders beneath the pale grey jacket, on the tall familiarity of him. She had missed him. Very much. Foolish tears filled her eyes. Jago seemed so dear, so welcome, she needed to fight an impulse to rush down and throw herself into his arms. Erin blinked and began to descend. She had almost reached the foot of the staircase before she spoke.

'How was New York?'

He jumped. 'What are you doing here?' he demanded, swivelling.

'Working late. Sorry if I startled you.' She noticed a bleakness around his mouth, a tension in the angular planes of his jaw. 'What's the matter?' she enquired anxiously. 'Have you got a headache?'

'Yes—you!'

Her hand went for the banister. Erin needed its support. Anger, cold as an Arctic blast, was filling the hall, sending shivers down her spine. He knows I've met Susie, she thought, recognising the man two steps below as the Ice Man.

'I used my time in New York to think—about you and me,' Jago grated, launching into an immediate attack. He slid his hands into his trouser pockets, placed his feet apart. 'I decided I was going to tell you about Susie, about a lot of other things, too. Not for publication, of course, but because I wanted to *share*.' He hurled the word at her like a harpoon. 'It isn't often I share things. Somehow it's always been taken for granted I'm the strong man in control, and strong men aren't supposed to admit to worries, to confess they wake up in the night scared stiff and in a cold sweat. However, I decided I could talk to you. Your intelligence and stability impressed me, made me think you'd understand. I even thought you might help!'

'I'd——' Erin's throat needed to be cleared before any reasonable sound could emerge. 'I'd like to help, to share.'

'Wouldn't you just! So long as it was a three-way share—me, you and that goddamn profile. It fills your mind to the extent that nothing else matters. In its name you're perfectly happy to give the nod to a dirty trick or two, or three, or four!' His laugh was bitter and disgusted. 'Why did I ever allow Burt to persuade me you were different? Why did I ever think you could be trusted? You softened me up real good, and I fell for it. Because you looked after me, made me that omelette, washed my hair—and bloody kissed me as though you meant it!—I believed you cared. Oh, not about me as Jago Miles, an actor whose life might make an hour's agreeable reading, but cared about me as *me*. How wrong I was!' His whole body vibrated with hostility. 'Writer, journalist, what the hell? You're a shark and without ethics like most of your media buddies.'

'I'm not. I——'

He allowed no entry. 'Today filming finished sooner than expected, so I caught an earlier flight. Having been gifted with some free time I decided to go and surprise my kid sister. Guess what? *I* had the surprise.' His blue eyes scratched a frosty path over her. 'Do you receive backhanders from the C.I.A.?' he demanded. 'It wouldn't surprise me to discover you're on their payroll. My God, I've heard of snoopers in my time, but——'

'I wasn't snooping, I wasn't,' Erin broke in, desperate to state her case. 'I came across Susie by chance. The only reason I went to the hospital in the first place was because you'd hurt your head.'

'And Florence Nightingale changed into private dick mid-stream?' he sneered. 'You can do better than that.'

'But I had no idea Susie, as a patient, existed.'

'You knew the hospital existed. Marvin made it very clear it was you who insisted I went there.'

'Someone had mentioned it, and—and I remembered,' she said stiffly.

'Someone? Which someone?' He shifted his stance, like a bull pawing the ground. 'Tell me!' he thundered.

Her hand tightened on the banister. 'Maria.'

'I bet! What reason would Maria have for mentioning that particular establishment? You make a big thing out of how you tell the truth in your writing, why not have a shot at telling the truth now?'

'I am. And if I make a big thing out of writing the truth, so you make an even bigger one out of keeping secrets. Do you think no one ever wondered about your hush-hush Wednesdays? Of course they did, it's a natural reaction,' she continued, when he was slow to answer. Erin frowned. The housekeeper's name had been forced from her, but Maria's involvement ended there. She refused to incriminate her. 'Apparently a tradesman reported how he'd seen you heading in the direction of the hospital.'

'This news was served up along with the coffee?'

Her chin lifted. 'No, I asked. You granted permission for me to ask questions and——'

'I didn't grant permission for you to employ the third degree,' Jago hissed.

She felt uneasy. 'It wasn't the third degree. It was one question. A legitimate enquiry.'

'Legitimate? Like hell!'

'How do you expect me to write an in-depth profile when one-seventh of your life's a blank?' Erin challenged, refusing to admit her query to Maria had been less than justified. She executed a rapid change of course. 'The nurse on reception was responsible for bringing Susie and me together. She suggested I might like to meet your young lady while I was waiting for you to be patched up.'

'You could have said no,' he slammed back.

'But—but it was fate,' she replied, wishing he wasn't making it sound as though she had committed a crime.

'My God, now I've heard everything.'

'It just—just happened,' she faltered, her heart thumping inside her breast like a jackhammer. She *had* done the right thing, she told herself. She *had* acted from the most worthwhile motives. There was no reason to buckle beneath his criticism. Yet the doubts which had once surfaced began to pinprick again.

'Happened? What you mean is you regarded the nurse on reception as heaven-sent. She must have been the one on duty today. She called to me as I was passing. She wanted to talk about my young lady, only this time she was referring to *you*. She said did I know how lucky I was to have found such a caring person?' He lifted his eyes to the ceiling 'Oh boy! She went on at great lengths, telling me how kind you'd been, going in to see my sister every day while I was away.'

'But I've enjoyed visiting Susie.'

'There was never any doubt about that,' he taunted. 'After all, what does Erin Page enjoy more than furthering the fortunes of her book? The unfortunate part is that although Susie knew you were interested in gathering information, she also believed you went as a friend.'

'I did!' Her voice squeaked in protest. 'I like her.'

'You like *pumping* her.'

'You're putting entirely the wrong slant on this. Yes, I did ask questions, but——'

'You sneaked in to see my sister behind my back. You arranged for your visits to be kept a secret. Your sole motivation in going to the hospital was your book!'

Her stomach churned. It was obvious Jago felt she had betrayed him, but she hadn't. Wasn't a successful book in his interests as well as hers, and ultimately in Susie's? Royalties would help finance her house. Rapidly Erin assembled a defence.

'You're wrong. For a start sneaking in sounds like I shinned up a drainpipe, but all that happened was the nurse rang through of her own volition, and Susie wanted to see me.'

'She would. When you've been stuck in a controlled environment for ages you don't turn away a new face.'

'Did you really tell her I was a knock-out intellectual?' she enquired.

'What's that apropos of?' he scowled.

'Nothing. Did you?'

'Yes. What I neglected to mention was your volatile streak! Don't sidetrack. The fact is you knew how I'd kept my visits secret, so you knew my so-called young lady was none of your goddamn business,' Jago said grimly. 'Why the hell couldn't you have stayed in reception until I came, and then asked me who she was?'

'Would you have told me?'

'Probably not.'

Erin moved a hand. 'There you are.'

'Where? Unlike you I don't subscribe to the belief that all's fair when it comes to love, war and writing books.'

'Neither do I.'

'No?'

'No.' Instead of churning, her stomach felt hollow. 'As far as keeping quiet about my visits was concerned, it was a temporary arrangement,' she said, flailing around in the hope of recapturing shreds of what was now a fast-disappearing confidence.

'I know, Susie explained. She explained *everything*. She didn't want to, but I——'

'You weren't rough on her?' Erin implored. 'Most of what she told me confirmed your account of your childhood, that's all. And in biographical terms two sources are always better than one.'

'Biographical terms?' He chewed on the phrase and spat it out. 'So we're harping on our book again, are we? It's always the damned book. Don't I remember you saying *Taro Beach* was just something on celluloid? Well, this all-consuming passion of yours is just black marks on paper, and does not excuse your actions.' His eyes signalled disgust. 'Not one iota!'

Erin felt queasy. No pinpricks, those doubts had begun to stab. Her grounds for visiting Susie had seemed so sturdy, but had she been mentally manipulating her reasons into an acceptable form? Jago's condemnation made horrible sense. Could absorption in her work have sucked her into overstepping the mark? Was she guilty of sharp practice? No. Maybe. *Yes*. It was a daunting realisation. Erin wished a crevasse would open and gobble her up. She drew a breath.

'You're right. I was wrong to have visited Susie without your permission,' she admitted. 'At the time I did wonder if I should, but——'

'So there wasn't just a blind belief that what you were doing was right?' he cut in. 'Well maybe there's hope for you yet. Where is this profile of yours?' he demanded suddenly.

From rock bottom, her spirits soared. Jago was

interested. All was not lost. Once he read what she'd written he would forgive and understand. He would agree that, on this occasion, the end did justify the means.

'It's upstairs. Come and have a look,' she offered eagerly, and when he joined her, she smiled. 'It's a first draft and incomplete, so please don't expect much. There are alterations, crossings out, and not much polish, but you should be able to get the flavour.'

The look he flung suggested the flavour might well be cyanide. Jago accompanied her into the back bedroom, where he straddled a chair and waited impatiently as she opened her briefcase.

'I hope you like it,' Erin said, handing over the manuscript as though handing over the Crown jewels. Jago frowned down. He's not going to read it! she panicked, in a taut moment when he remained immobile. Then he began to thumb through. 'Chapter Five's the one which refers to Susie,' she burbled, relief making her loquacious. 'And if you're wondering, I haven't included Olivia.'

In response she received a steely glare.

'I don't know why I'm doing this,' he muttered.

At first his inspection was cursory, then a sentence caught his eye. Jago read a little, and in time turned to Chapter Five. A paragraph was scanned here, a comment frowned over there. Please let him like it, Erin prayed. This piecemeal scrutiny was not the long leisurely read she had planned for Saturday, yet surely he would recognise how Susie and her disability had been handled in an understated and sensible manner? The minutes dragged on. A clock ticked somewhere. No use attempting to read anything from his expression, for Jago was poker-faced. Erin felt as if she was growing into an old, old lady.

'Well?' she breathed, when finally he raised his head.

'Very good.'

She sank back. 'Thank you.'

'That doesn't mean it can be published.'

She jerked upright. 'Why ever not?'

'Erin, I've kept my sister away from the media for well over two years now,' he said heavily.

She waited for more, for a fuller explanation. Nothing came. 'That's it?' she asked.

'Isn't it enough?' She shook her head. 'Well, it's all you're getting.'

Why was he so belligerent, so guarded? This desire to protect Susie was overdone, did not make sense.

'What possible harm can a little exposure do?' she appealed. 'And it is a little.'

'No.'

'Jago, the public——'

'If you intend to quote jargon about the public having a right to know, forget it. It's rhetoric. It means nothing.'

'I was going to say that the public are not ogres,' she said tersely. 'Look, if guilt's involved in this, it shouldn't be.'

'Guilt?' he questioned.

Abruptly, she was stumbling. 'If—if you feel guilty about the crash.'

'I don't.' Jago frowned at the bundle in his hand. 'This can't go ahead as it stands.'

'But if the reference to Susie's picked up and some publicity results, she won't mind. She's said she won't. I think she'd enjoy it. That girl has spunk. She's well adjusted and——'

'No,' he bit out, his face darkening.

'You mollycoddle her far too much. Her body might not be perfect, but her mind is. She can cope, she——'

'No.'

'Any publicity would be a nine-day wonder.'

'No.'

'Can't you be something else but negative?' she flared. Erin had tried all the angles she could think of, and each time come up against a solid brick wall. 'Can't you see reason?'

'Can't you see further than your goddamn book?'

Her jaw tightened. 'You should be grateful for my goddamn book. If *Taro Beach* finishes you may well need the money it'll bring in.'

'*Taro Beach* is finishing, confirmation came through while I was in New York. So yes, I'll need the money, but not from this.' He rapped the sheaf of paper with his knuckles. 'Any royalties will be from the next profile you write—a different one— one which complies with my wishes. I've provided plenty of first-hand information, so there shouldn't be any problems. Leaving Susie out isn't going to——'

'I don't want to write a different profile.'

'Exactly. You want to write what you want to write. That's why Edwardians are tailor-made. They can't squawk if you go too far.'

'I don't go too far. I write the truth, which is what I want to do now.'

'You will.'

'The *complete* truth.'

Jago raked a hand through his hair. 'You're not a shark, you're a terrier clinging on to a bone. Sorry, but you're going to have to let go. Tomorrow you can start on a fresh profile.'

Erin glared. 'Suppose I refuse?'

'You mean it's this or nothing?'

The earth juddered beneath her feet. Juddered and went still. 'Yes,' she announced impetuously.

'Then it's nothing.' Jago flung the chair out from under him. 'Forget you ever met me, because I'm damn well going to forget I ever met you.' With the papers clutched in his hand, he headed for the door. 'The only thing to do with this is to burn it.'

'Burn? Burn my manuscript?' she spluttered, gazing at him in wide-eyed disbelief.

'Why not? It's of no use any more.'

'But you mustn't! You wouldn't! You can't!' Erin flew across the room. 'Give it to me.'

His raised his arm, holding the cargo high above his head. 'You think I'm fool enough to let you take this back to England?'

'It's *my* property.'

'It's *my* life. If I say it goes up in flames, then go up in flames it does. I don't want this kind of private information kicking around. As long as it does, how can I rest easy? For all I know you might decide to sell the story to——'

'I wouldn't! I wouldn't sell it to anyone,' Erin rejected hotly. She lunged upwards, but the papers remained tantalisingly beyond her reach. 'I'm not an opportunist.'

'No, you're not,' he agreed with a frown. 'What

the hell are you? Money and fame aren't the motivations, so what makes Erin tick?' Jago switched the manuscript to his other hand, thwarting her. 'It's blatantly clear you use your writing as a dumping ground for all the emotions you should be using elsewhere, but why?'

'Give me that manuscript!'

He stepped aside to avoid her thrashing arms. 'What happens if you board the plane without it—the world falls apart? This isn't the Holy Grail. You aren't an emissary on a divine mission.'

'I want it.' Erin pushed brown curls back from a forehead which had become flushed and clammy. '*Please.*'

'No. You'll feel much better when this has gone, when it's out of your system. You need to be exorcised, then perhaps you can start to live again—live properly.' He fended off her grabbing hand. 'Hell, my career's important to me, but I don't devote my entire existence to it to the exclusion of everything else.'

She thumped a fist on his chest. 'Give me my manuscript.'

'It's of no use.'

'I don't care, I want it.'

Erin threw herself forward, clawing and flailing, but was held off with infuriating ease. How could she make him hand over *her* property? Leaping up and down was futile, thumping at his chest wasn't doing much good either. But the manuscript was hers, hers, *hers*. She lifted her foot and slammed it into his ankle as hard as she could.

'You——' Jago cringed, swore viciously, then flicked his wrist. He sent the papers skimming across the room to where they landed, dead centre of the water-bed. 'Wait!' he commanded before she could leap for retrieval, and the authority in his voice acted like a leash. 'Behave like a bitch, get treated like one. You sit and you stay, and you listen to me.'

He had indicated a chair behind the desk. Erin glowered. There was a moment of hesitation in which she weighed up her survival if she rebelled, but a look at his face said retribution would be swift and uncompromising. Jago in this mood was not to be treated lightly. She went and sat down. In turn Jago limped to his own chair, straddling it again. His ankle was rubbed, frowned over, then he lifted his head.

'Don't imagine you have a monopoly on determination,' he said. 'Ever since I kissed you I've wanted you. I still do, which, considering the present circumstances, seems remarkable. However, I appear to be lumbered with a libido which has a will of its own. Which means——' the blue eyes narrowed to slits '— that if you get on that bed and touch that manuscript, then I get on that bed and I touch you.'

Her stomach tightened. Erin heard a ringing in her ears. 'You—you'd rape me?' she gasped.

Slowly he shook his head. 'It wouldn't be rape, would it? Oh, maybe you'd fight a little, but you'd soon surrender. We both know that. You gave yourself away at the beach when your lips clung to mine just a moment too long, when you stayed on top of me. Would you like to lie on top of me again, with us both naked this time?' His voice had become silk and smoke. 'Would you like to feel my mouth on your breast, know the ecstasy when I part your thighs?'

Erin lowered her lids. 'Don't,' she begged.

'Why not allow me to introduce you to the joys of making love on a water-bed? The drifting feeling adds a whole new dimension to intimacy. It'll bring out the best in both of us and your best, Erin my sweet, could be very, very good.' He stretched out a large hand. 'Shall we?'

'No!' she yelped. She was aroused enough with him talking like this. Whatever happened, Jago must not touch her.

'It would be a memorable way to say goodbye, and especially for you. After all, you have been leading a hellishly boring life.'

'Have I?'

'Haven't you?' he drawled. 'If I was in your shoes I'd leap at this chance of some action.'

He was so condescending, so supremely in charge, so inviolate, that something inside her snapped.

'You think I haven't known much *action*?' Erin demanded.

Jago moved wide shoulders. 'I think there's a good chance you and your husband were virgins on your wedding day, and that due to such a short time together the sex never got to be too fantastic. Never mind, I can——'

'You can what?' she interrupted, in a brittle voice. 'Enlighten a small-town girl? Open up a whole, new, wonderful world? Sorry to disappoint, but you've been picking up faulty signals. My sexual education was completed six years ago by another actor, so I don't require extra tuition. Ned taught me how to press all the right buttons, ring all the right chimes, and I was a fast learner. Very fast!' Her chin jutted. 'We made love night and day, and never in bed with the lights switched off. Ned had far more energy and imagination than to be content with that!' She flung Jago a caustic glance. 'So you see, I know precisely what kind of a gift my sensuality is. And yes, you're right, I would surrender because you attract me as Ned attracted me. You're both big and blond and——' she gave a strangled sob, '— bastards.'

'Erin——' He rose from his seat.

'Leave me alone!'

The shame of what had happened so long ago erupted inside her like a volcano and those tears came flooding down her face. Hot tears. Unstoppable tears. Tears which needed to be shed. Head in her hands, she sat there and sobbed while Jago looked on impotently.

'Erin, I'm not Ned,' he insisted, when the racking sobs gradually lessened.

'No, you're not.' She blew her nose, wiped her wet cheeks. She shuddered. 'I want to apologise. I should never have gone to see Susie without first clearing it with you, and I should never have bowled on and included her in the profile. I guess I knew all along my behaviour was ... irregular.' Red-eyed and still shuddering, she struggled to compose herself. 'Somehow my writing gave me tunnel vision, and I seemed able to justify anything.' She swallowed. 'Now I'd like to wipe the slate clean and begin again. I can write a perfectly acceptable account of your life without any reference to Susie and, if you agree, I'll start on it tomorrow.'

Jago smiled. 'I agree. Shall we seal the bargain?' He held out his hand. This time she took it.

CHAPTER EIGHT

SUCH a thorough shake-up left Erin bruised and battered. Tight-closed corners of her mind had been wrenched open and in consequence her lifestyle, aims, hopes; her present and her future—everything—needed to be reassessed. Now she understood that whilst her writing had provided a necessary survival kit following the trauma of Ned, over the years it had moved in and taken control. The time for her to control *it* was long overdue. Channelling all her energies, creative and otherwise, into a single stream smacked of obsession, not the dedication she had previously congratulated herself upon. When had she last gone on holiday, taken an interest in buying new furnishings for the cottage, picked flowers, even raised her eyes from her typewriter to marvel at the colours of a sunset? These were omissions which needed to be rectified, urgently.

And what about the Edwardian biography planned to come next? Maybe the idea should be scrapped and she should stick with writing about today's people, today's world? Cleo would approve, for it had been her agent's dogged determination, not her own impetus, which had lifted this current book off the ground.

'Stop vegetating in libraries, kick the habit of poring over dusty documents at home,' Cleo had implored. 'Your Edwardians will keep. I've trundled out this suggestion before—like on fifty separate occasions!—but why not have a bash at a sequel to your women book? From a personal standpoint making contact with the living has to pay dividends. And along the way try to grab some fun, maybe even fall in love, there's a good girl.'

Fun and love, where were they? Such commodities seemed to have been in short supply. Although she had dated over the past six years, it had been sparingly and always with men who made few demands on both her time and her body. Erin had not been aware of choosing escorts for these reasons, but now she began to wonder. And where were the husband and babies she had once visualised? In the past she had been smug, informing herself that whereas any dimwit could have a family, only the sacred few were capable of producing a book. Besides, she had plenty of time to find someone to love. That time had dwindled. She was thirty. Not ancient exactly, but lagging behind her friends who were well established with husbands, plus one, two, even three children. Once her books had seemed far superior to any husband, any child. Now they seemed to be—just books.

Yet how did she set about restructuring her life? Fun was no problem; in the month which followed that solved itself—thanks to a lively nature which was now allowed free and varied expression. And thanks to Jago. On seeing how promptly she had sought to set her work in a less intense context, he had made a positive response. Over the past four weeks they had swum together in the pool, strolled along the seashore, whooshed around on his motorbike—this last pastime resulting in Erin becoming almost an addict herself. Despite these

excursions, the profile had not suffered. Jago had
fed the remainder of his career into her tape
recorder, while she had kept pace with the writing.
Erin had discovered afresh how work can be
harmoniously combined with pleasure.

On Wednesdays they had visited the hospital.
Jago had been insistent she join him and, though
apprehensive, she had agreed. Apprehension
proved superfluous. There were no recriminations.
Within seconds of her meeting Susie again, a joke
had been cracked and the three of them had
laughed. Erin could relax. The visits, like the
swimming, the strolling, the bike riding, had been
fun.

That left love. To her bewilderment, Jago had not
made a positive response there. On the contrary, the
blond Viking with a glint in his eye had switched to
being ultra-correct, ultra-proper, ultra-platonic.
There had been ample opportunities for him to give
rein to that wayward libido, but he had ignored
them all. Admittedly there were moments when
Erin wondered if—hoped that—the sparkle which
joined them might be attributed to something more
than a cheery companionship, but when he continued to keep his distance these had had to be
dismissed as figments of her imagination.

She could only assume the revelation of her affair
with Ned had brought about this change. Jago's
interest had been piqued by a woman he had
considered unschooled in the ways of love, but once
alerted to the fact she was a member of the
cognoscenti, albeit a lapsed member, his interest had
fizzled. Not that he was aloof. He was so damned
amiable Erin was tempted to lash out at his ankle

again and demand to know what he thought he was playing at. 'Brother, protector, friend, father—all rolled into one' had been Susie's description, and now it so aptly applied to his attitude towards *her*.

But she didn't want Jago as a brother or as anything else platonic. She wanted him to acknowledge her as the sensual woman he had insisted she was. She wanted him to . . . Erin sighed, conscious of the unrelenting tick of time. What did it matter what she wanted? This Sunday was her final day in Florida and already it was evening. Tomorrow, as Jago travelled to Miami to complete the penultimate episode of *Taro Beach*, she would board a plane to fly up, up and away into the wide blue sky. Chances were they would never meet again.

'You're very quiet, toots,' Jago remarked, drawing Burt's Cadillac to a halt beside the toll booth. He stretched to fiddle in his trouser pocket for coins, then tossed them into the basket. Seconds later they were heading across the causeway towards the island. 'Has the sunshine worn you out? Never mind, it's added the finishing touch to a wonderful tan.' He surveyed her, smiling. In a sleeveless pistachio-green shirt and brief shorts, Erin was a creature of honey-brown limbs. 'You'll be a sensation back home. You'll bring the traffic to a complete standstill.'

'Will I?' she said wistfully, thinking she would rather be a sensation here, bring him to a standstill. 'I am tired,' she agreed. 'It's been a busy day.'

They had started early. Commandeering Burt's air-conditioned Cadillac for the long ride in preference to the bike, they had driven north to an aquatic theme park in central Florida. There Jago had donned the requisite sunglasses and flat cap, and wandered with her incognito. The day had been a parade of delights. They had applauded performing dolphins, sea-lions, starched-front penguins. Visited aquariums, watched dancing fountains, laughed themselves silly at a water-skiing pig. They had been able to enjoy themselves like any other anonymous young couple for, in all those hours, Jago had been recognised just once. Several questioning glances had come his way, but as no one expected a TV heart-throb to mix with the *hoi polloi*, and especially dressed in last year's jeans and an unprepossessing checked shirt, those glances had skated on. Only a little girl, braces silvering her teeth, had seen through his disguise. Sidling up, she had patted his knee for attention and when he had bent down had whispered shyly into his ear, 'I love you, Jago Miles.'

A lump blocked Erin's throat. It had been a busy day. A busy day for thinking. As time ran out, minute by minute, hour by hour, her feelings had crystallised. 'I love you, Jago Miles.' Now she knew those were the words she wanted to say. But what would happen if she did? At a guess she'd be awarded a quick squeeze and have her hair tousled, like the little girl. Why must Jago choose now to manifest this old-fashioned sense of propriety? she wondered in disgust. Why couldn't he have suggested they embark on a red-hot love affair? She would not have resisted. Indeed, there was a distinct probability she would have been across the room, sitting on his knee, before he had completed the first sentence. Erin shifted in her seat. This was zigzag logic. Completely slain she might be; a lover, live-in or any other species, she was not.

'The theme park was great,' she added, careless of the stretched pause since her last remark. 'Susie would have loved it.'

'Yeah, especially the killer whale,' he agreed, and began to relive the events of the day.

Water which had shimmered blue on either side of the causeway was replaced by wafting palms; now they were on the island. Jago continued to reminisce, but Erin wasn't listening. All she could think about was that in less than five minutes' time they were destined to reach the Driftwood Motel. In less than five minutes, they would make the appropriate noises and say goodbye. Everything would be over. Five minutes shrank into three, two, and still Jago yammered on. Erin's muscles contracted. She clasped her arms across her stomach. Whatever existed between the two of them, its death seemed to be more than she could bear. At the sight of the low white motel, bathed golden in the setting sun, she cringed. Dimly she became aware of Jago tacking a query on to a comment about the antics of the water-skiing pig.

'How in hell's name do I finance Susie's house?' he asked, and she shot him a look of astonishment.

The amiable distance of the past four weeks had meant that nothing which could be remotely described as 'personal' had ever been discussed. Osmosis had not been needed to absorb that whilst they might be friends, Jago remained disinclined to share. Any problems were his, something he dealt with alone. Yet here he was, asking a question and looking to her for an answer.

'You don't,' she replied, sloughing off her

melancholy. 'Next time you visit the hospital you come clean about *Taro Beach* folding and explain that a custom-built property is far beyond your means.'

The speedometer needle flickered and fell. Jago swung the Cadillac on to the motel forecourt and steered into the appropriate slot outside her room.

'No,' he argued, as he cut the engine. 'No, I——'

'If you intend to borrow money and go into debt again, you're mad,' Erin informed him crisply. 'Look what happened before. In order to stay afloat you were forced to accept a role in a tacky soap opera.'

'What else could I do?' he protested, a tightness around his mouth giving clear indication that such bluntness was neither expected nor desired.

'Nothing, then. It's different now, crisis time is over. Agreed you have responsibilities towards Susie, but you also have them towards yourself. Shouldn't they be considered? You're a fine actor, Jago, yet step on that financial treadmill again and you could end up squandering your talent for ever and a day.'

'But——'

'But Susie has her heart set on a dream house and she'll be disappointed if it doesn't materialise? I know. I agree. But she'll understand. Not instantly, not like that.' Erin snapped her fingers. 'But after a while, when the first disappointment's over and everything has had a chance to be digested. Personally I think leaving her to wallow in Cloud-Cuckoo-Land is both shortsighted and unfair.' The tightness around his mouth had been joined by a scowl. She ignored them both. So often she had been on the brink of voicing her misgivings about the attitude he adopted with his sister and now— well, he had asked for an opinion. If that opinion wasn't what he wanted to hear—tough! 'Susie deserves access to the facts,' she continued. 'Irrespective of whether or not she's sitting in a wheelchair, she's an adult. Why not start treating her like one? You do no one a favour by pussyfooting around. The sooner she knows the true situation, the sooner she can get to grips with it. And it's time you realised she's interpreted your reluctance to commit to a property as an aversion to Robert.'

'I like the guy,' Jago retorted. 'I've told her so.'

'You can tell her until you're blue in the face, but until she receives an honest explanation of why you're holding back, she won't believe you. She's far too perceptive to be fobbed off.' Erin's tone softened. 'Listen, instead of mumbling about how the pair of them are in too much of a hurry, why not confess you're no longer Mr Rockefeller?'

He pulled a face. 'I guess that makes some kind of sense,' he admitted.

'It makes *real* sense. And if being told a de luxe villa isn't available is disappointing, it's scarcely a major disaster. More of a setback. Both Susie and Robert are capable of handling a setback. They don't need to be pampered, they don't *want* to be pampered,' she insisted, as Jago tugged at his ear. 'Leastways Robert doesn't, and in the long run won't what agrees with him find agreement with Susie? As it is he's dubious about receiving handouts. Maybe he can't walk and he can't run, but he's just as much a man as you are. He has his pride. And

whilst he accepts the need for some assistance, some
support, he gags at the prospect of largesse being
stuffed down his throat.'

'Then what would you suggest I do? Let me lay
my resources on the line,' he continued, exhibiting a
sudden willingness to open up. 'I have near enough
seventy thousand dollars in the bank and there's
also a residue of my *Taro Beach* salary yet to come.
That's the good news.' Jago sighed. 'The bad news
is there are some medical fees still outstanding and
the possibility I could be out of work for—
perpetuity.'

'So how can you assess how much is needed to
support yourself for an unknown number of rainy
days?' Erin was thinking aloud. 'It's tricky.'

'Suppose I split the money straight down the
middle?' he suggested.

'Good idea,' she agreed. 'That would enable you
to explain your predicament to Susie and Robert,
and follow up with the offer of a set amount towards
the purchase of a more modest house, an existing
one which could be economically adapted to suit
their needs. Then Robert can find the remainder of
the purchase price himself. He can, he's told me he's
able to raise a fairly robust loan,' she explained.
'And if he's responsible for the lion's share it'd be
perfect, because then he'll rightfully be in a position
to consider himself the owner!'

Jago grinned at her triumphant tone. 'So all that's
needed now is for Susie to be dissuaded from setting
her sights on anything too ambitious, like the White
House.'

'I know she enjoys company, but guided tours
marching through morning, noon and night? Come

off it. If you like I could prod my publishers to see if they'll cough up an advance from your royalties,' Erin offered.

'Thanks. If those rainy days turn out to be the monsoon season I shall need all the help I can get.' Jago eased himself lower in the seat. Talk of rainy days he might, yet his grin had not been dislodged. It was the kind of grin which could have electrified if she hadn't recognised it as the infuriatingly amiable grin of a brother, protector, etc. etc. 'I know it's crazy,' he said, 'but for weeks now I've been knotted up over Susie and her goddamned house, and all of a sudden everything seems— manageable.' He reached out for Erin's hand and brought it to his mouth. 'Thanks for being such a great unraveller,' he murmured.

His tone was teasing, the look in his eyes was not. Brother *et al* flew out of the window. The pressure of his lips had Erin feeling heated and ruffled. Why decide now that I merit attention as something more than a buddy? she groaned inwardly. Now is too late.

'Pleased to be of service, sir,' she quipped, extracting her hand to administer a flippant salute. She avoided his eyes. If she wasn't careful the power in them would have her melting into a puddle. 'Is a plan of action organised for when *Taro Beach* grinds to a halt?' she asked, matter-of-factly.

'I can't see what else to do apart from hawking myself around. Unless you have a better suggestion?'

She had several. Like him coming to live in her cottage, like him allowing her to whisk him off to the kasbah, like her using him as her plaything.

' 'Fraid not,' she said.

'Oh well.'

Jago shrugged. He removed the ignition key and began to toy with it. He shifted his hips in the seat, grew restless. In contrast, Erin froze. Goodbye time, that dreaded time, had arrived. He was preparing a farewell. But how could she sit meekly and listen? No way. She lurched for the door handle. She couldn't find it. Where had the stupid thing gone? She found it and, pressing down to open the door, she turned.

'Jago——'

'Erin——' he said simultaneously. They both laughed. 'Do you have a copy of your book on women?' he asked.

'Yes, in my suitcase. Cleo insisted I bring one. I think she feels I ought to waft it around like an advertisement. Why? Would—would you like to read it?' she enquired, thinking that he left everything to the last minute.

'I already have. You didn't think I'd expose myself to you without taking the precaution of examining your credentials?' he teased, when she looked surprised. 'Enchanted with your big brown eyes and long legs I might be, but I do retain tatters of common sense. Burt obtained a copy at the very start of our collaboration.'

'Oh.' Enchanted with her eyes and her legs, was he? But it was too late, too late, too damned *late*. 'Er—did you approve?' Erin thought to enquire.

'Very much, but there's something I'd like to check.'

'I'll get the book.'

'I'll come with you.'

She dived out of the car. 'There's no need, really.'

'There's every need, really.' He shone a smile across the roof of the Cadillac. 'Or do the management have rules which state that men caught entering the rooms of unattached young ladies will be castrated?'

Erin blushed. 'The management is very good,' she said, hastily elbowing the conversation on to a less disturbing line. 'They train their staff well here. Everyone's pleasant, the service is excellent.' She unlocked her door. 'I've been very comfortable here. As you can see there's plenty of space. The air-conditioning is quiet, an electric kettle and coffee bags are provided, and——'

'Don't tell me. The towels are changed twice a day?'

In confusion she dropped to her knees and began a rapid search through the half-packed suitcase. Clothes which had been folded with care were now flung aside. She found the book, handed it up. 'What is it you want to check? she enquired.

'A name.'

'Oh.'

Yet another inane 'oh'. For a wordsmith her vocabulary was surprisingly limited. Erin rose to her feet. She longed to know which of the four profiles he was leafing through, longed to know which name he could possibly want to check, but Jago had withdrawn to a couple of yards away.

When he found the page he wanted he gave her a sombre glance.

' "But forget Lady Macbeth and Blanche in *A Streetcar Named Desire*, the role closest to Patrice's heart has always been the one of mother",' he read.

Erin was mortified. She remembered what came next, remembered only too well. Metaphorically Jago had placed his hands around her neck and was in the process of throttling her. ' "Edward, her only child, whilst not born in the proverbial trunk, did spend much of his youth in and around the theatre",' he continued. ' "This was a useful apprenticeship for now he is successfully following in his mother's footsteps." ' The book snapped closed. 'Edward Lanham,' he said, thrusting the name at her. 'He's Ned.'

The pink in her cheeks became a dull rose. 'Yes.'

'What happened?'

'I've told you.'

'No. All I learned from your outburst a month ago was that while you regard the man as your enemy now, at one time you and he were two people madly, impetuously in love.'

Erin's head went down. She stared at the carpet. Woven with a diamond pattern, each shape was outlined in dark amber, the inside a paler shade. Carpet, curtains and bedspread were all amber-hued, while the bedroom walls were white. Her eyes followed a diamond from one point, to the next, the next, the next.

'It wasn't two people,' she muttered. 'It was one. Just me.'

'What happened?' Jago repeated.

'If you don't mind, I'd——'

'I do mind. I want to know.' Tossing the book into the suitcase, he caught hold of her chin. Thumb and fingers spread, he raised her head until she was forced to meet his gaze. 'You can't keep everything bottled up inside for all time.'

'Who says I have?' she attacked.

'Erin, in six years who have you told about your affair?'

'Cleo. Well, she knows parts.' She felt agitated, fractious. 'I'm not ready to talk.'

'After six years? Come on. You're ready. You *are* ready.'

Was she? Six years of silence suddenly struck her as—obsessive. She had been obsessive about her writing, and that was wrong. Wasn't keeping quiet about Ned equally a fault? Tucking a strand of hair behind her ear, Erin decided she would talk. What did she have to lose? She knew Jago would despise her when he heard what she had to say, but it didn't really matter because in a few hours' time she would be gone.

'I met Ned through his mother, obviously,' she said, and Jago stepped back, releasing her. 'I'd gone to London and——' Erin broke off. If this was her confessional, honesty demanded she set everything very clearly in the correct time scale, no matter how shaming that time scale might be. She started again, gesturing towards the discarded book. 'I'd completed two of those profiles when Peter's illness was first diagnosed. Naturally writing fell by the wayside and after his death I couldn't seem to summon up the will to start again. Cleo left me alone for a while, then came to see me. She explained how the publishers were chary of leaving the project hanging and asked if there was a chance of me completing the book, like as of now. She pointed out that having something else to think about would be beneficial, and I had to agree. Patrice Lanham's profile was the next one scheduled, so I made contact.' Erin sank down on the bed. 'She welcomed me with open arms. It was "dahling" this and "sweetie-pie" that, and although I accepted much of it was affectation, I gained the impression she liked me. When she suggested I move into her house while we worked together, I was happy to agree.' She scowled. 'No, I wasn't happy, that's a gross understatement. I was so damned *pleased*, that when I think of it now I want to curl up and die.'

'Ned lived in the house, too?'

She nodded. 'Patrice is divorced from her third husband, so it was just the two of them. A great double act!'

'He began to pay court?'

Erin gave a bleak laugh. 'Nothing so restrained. He marched into my room one night, a week or so after I'd moved in and calmly advised me we were made for each other. He'd never believed in love at first sight, but then he'd met me. I was the half which would make him whole. This thing is bigger than both of us.' Her mouth became a harsh line. 'All the tired old phrases poured out, blah, blah, blah.'

'And?' Jago prompted, when she lapsed into a frowning silence.

'And I let him into my bed. Amazing, isn't it?' she demanded, waiting for a gasp of incredulity. None came. Instead, her companion folded his arms and rested a broad shoulder against the wall. 'I could hardly believe it myself,' Erin continued, knowing that although outwardly noncommittal, inside Jago must be shocked to the core. 'One minute I was telling him to get out of my room and protesting I hardly knew him, the next——' Disgust coarsened her voice. 'The whole thing was like a dream, now it seems like a nightmare. Peter was barely cold in his grave and there I was, kissing this stranger as though my life depended on it.'

'Perhaps it did.'

'What do you mean?' she demanded suspiciously.

'That you were raw, fragile, and in need of comfort.'

'But Peter had only been dead four months!' she cried. 'Four short months!'

'And you've whipped yourself with those months ever since?'

Her eyes blazed. 'Shouldn't I?'

'No.' Jago moved, reaching down to place his hands on her shoulders. 'Erin, you were still in shock, lost and desperately lonely. At times like that the cuddle factor is of great importance.'

She looked away. 'It wasn't cuddles, it was sex. Pure unadulterated sex!'

'It was someone holding you close, murmuring endearments, someone cherishing you when you needed to be cherished.'

A tear escaped to roll down her cheek. 'I behaved like a slut.'

'Stop being so goddamn hard on yourself,' he protested, giving her a little shake. 'If a young widow responds to solace, who can blame her?'

'Solace from a man like Ned?' she derided. 'He was on television a while back and even a two-year-old would have spotted him for a phoney. The thing is, I think I always knew that, I just never would admit it to myself.'

'But at some time in our lives all of us are drawn towards someone we know is no good for us, yet we don't—can't—pull back. This Ned offered you cherishing, plus some excitement. A walk on the wild side, if you like.'

'I did like,' she said impatiently, 'but Peter——'

'Peter was dead, Ned was alive, that's the difference. One hell of a difference. Also he sounds to have been a demon lover. Your husband wasn't a demon lover, was he?'

'N—no,' she stammered, unprepared for this directness.

'But even so he'd awakened your sexuality. When he became ill, died, that sexuality continued to grow, like a bud opening in the grass. Along gallops Ned and you're ripe for the plucking.' Jago released her shoulders. 'How did his mother react to your love affair?'

'Like a cheerleader. Patrice was always hip-hip-hooraying. "Dahling, I've never seen Ned in such a tiz-woz. It'll be so cosy when you're my daughter-in-law, sweetie-pie" ', she mimicked. 'Not that Ned proposed, but with his mother banging the tambourine, who needed a proposal? I was so blind. The two of them were in league, buttering me up so I'd produce a favourable profile, and all the time I thought——' Erin nibbled at a fingernail. 'During the period I was their guest they must have been busy cementing Ned's friendship with the daughter of a theatrical impresario, the girl he married soon after. She was money in the bank where his career was concerned, while I——' Her voice cracked. 'I was disposable. I served my purpose and was then tossed out with the trash.'

'It's not a sin to make mistakes. The Lanhams were hard-boiled sophisticates while you——'

'I was the serving wench who slept with the young lord under the misapprehension one day he'd make me his lady?' she taunted. 'The irony is I *loved* sleeping with him.'

'Shouldn't you have done? Erin, sexuality is a part of human nature,' he said, in a distinct tone of exasperation. 'Maybe making whoopee with a skunk like Lanham wasn't rational, but at the time you weren't in a rational state of mind. He took advantage of that, plus the fact you possessed a normal, healthy appetite for sex. Yes, normal,' he stressed. 'If the beginning of a love affair isn't hot as in H O T,' Jago's mouth quirked, 'you can bet your bottom dollar something's wrong.'

That quirk made her mouth quirk, too. All of a sudden her past did not seem as dreadful as she had imagined. 'The steam certainly came out of my ears,' she said, and grinned. 'The day the completed profile went forward for publication was the day I got dumped. Ned took me out to dinner, and over the smoked salmon explained how driving fifty miles out into the countryside to see me could prove inconvenient. By the steak and green salad, it had become a distinct hitch. At the profiterole stage he damn near paralleled the journey to a trek to the North Pole. I retreated to my igloo, and two weeks later read of our reluctant explorer's engagement to the impresario's daughter.'

'Exit Mr Lanham, stage left?'

'Not quite. About a year later, when his wife was in the final throes of pregnancy, whose Mercedes should draw to a halt outside my garden gate but Ned's.'

'The North Pole had suddenly become

accessible?'

'It had become *the* place to visit,' she said drily.

'With his usual charm he explained how, of late, nostalgia had struck. He had such fond memories of our time together and he was wondering about us recreating some of our own private mayhem.' Erin lifted the rich fall of hair from the back of her neck, unconsciously arching. 'I thanked him politely for the suggestion, but advised that although once I may have possessed an altruistic bent, it did have its limits. Succouring errant husbands fell beyond them. Ned found that very hard to believe, so hard that I needed to point out a couple of his most glaring character defects before the message sank in.' She let the hair fall back to her shoulders. 'Seeing him again didn't do much for my sense of worth. I mean, if I had to behave disgracefully, why couldn't I have done so with somebody halfway decent?' She rose from the bed. 'Somebody like you.'

'I'm halfway decent?'

'All the way.' Erin took a step towards him, surprising herself with her boldness. 'Are you a demon lover?'

'Are you making a pass at me?' Jago countered, an amused brow lifting.

'Yes.' A pause. 'Do you mind?'

'Not in the least. The only reason I've been back-pedalling this past month is because I know you're in the middle of sorting yourself out, and it's something you must do without any outside influences.' He moved to meet her halfway. Reaching out long fingers, he pushed her shirt an inch or two back from her shoulder. He lowered his head, the tip of his tongue protruding. 'Tastes good,' he murmured as he licked the golden-brown flesh. 'Of sun and salt and Erin.'

'Better than tutti-frutti ice-cream?' she smiled, as her blood began its dizzy chase.

'Much better.' Jago opened his mouth and gently bit her shoulder. 'What happens next?' he asked, when she stood immobile. 'What do you want to happen next?' He pressed his lips to the faint crescents of teethmarks. 'Toots, sometimes you have to come right out and ask for what you want.'

Her heart fluttered. 'I'm—I'm scared.'

'After six years of playing safe, who wouldn't be?'

He straightened and began to rub his forehead against hers in slow motion, back and forth, back and forth. The rhythm soothed.

'I—I want a shower,' Erin got out. Eternity passed by. 'With you.'

'Then why are we wasting time?' He went to the window and closed the curtains. Coming back through the half-light he reminded her of a Nordic warrior, his hair shining like a blond helmet. 'I trust there isn't a no-nudity clause in your contract?' Jago murmured, as he eased her shirt from her shorts.

Slowly the garment was unbuttoned—slowly because kisses intervened—and then it was cast aside. Naked to the waist, Erin trembled. Yes, she was scared, but as he looked down on her that fear transformed itself into pride. She was proud the sight of her pleased him, proud their shared kisses had brought that glow to his eyes.

'You're beautiful,' Jago breathed. For a moment his eyes alone caressed her, then, as if her body held a fatal fascination, his hands joined in. Firm fingers slid up her ribcage until the silken smoothness of the underside of her breasts was being stroked. He cupped the full curves in his hands, rejoicing in their weight, their texture. 'Beautiful,' he sighed again. He had touched her tenderly, reverently, but a need was beginning to build. One hand wound into her rich dark curls. He pulled her against him and his mouth crushed down. Their tongues entwined, hotly, magically. His free hand returned to her breasts as though he *had* to feel, *had* to touch, had no choice but to roll a taut nipple urgently between the tips of his fingers until Erin gasped. The mouth on hers smiled.

Jago slid his hands down, pressing the shorts off over her hips. In like fashion lacy silk briefs were removed. Now he succumbed to an orgy of touching. His fingers moved from her shoulder-blades to her waist to the curve of her buttocks—feeling, moulding, possessing. 'Beautiful.' His hands came around, starting with her shoulders again but touring over the pout of her breasts, her stomach, across the triangle of brown moss to nudge between her thighs. Once again she gasped. Once again the mouth on hers smiled.

'It works both ways, honey,' he murmured. 'Feel what you've done to me?' Jago had said this before, but this time he took hold of her hand and steered it down between their bodies, leaving her in no doubt about his arousal.

'If it works both ways, you must be naked too,' Erin grinned, and working together they speedily removed his clothes.

Now she was free to press her fingers against the throbbing pulse, making Jago tremble, jerking back

his head in a muffled cry. He kissed her again, thick
and fast. The flames which for six years Erin had
feared, began to ignite. Vivid and orange-warm,
they licked over her body. More kisses, and her
hands began to move of their own accord, seeking
and finding pleasure in the width of his shoulders,
in the hair on his chest, returning to the hard virility
of his thighs. Jago shuddered, gave an incoherent
moan and then, their mouths still locked, steered
her across the room and into the shower.

The water's sting snatched away her breath. The
warm spray lashed down, slicking their heads to
gloss, creating rivulets which ran pell-mell over
their bodies like mountain torrents. Jago found the
soap and, as steam rose around them in white
clouds, began to massage her neck and shoulders.
The feeling was exquisite. Erin laughed, she sighed.
She kissed him fiercely, wetly, and murmured her
delight. His hands moved lower, drawn to the
luscious curves. He began soaping her breasts in
firm, sweeping movements, allowing his palms to
caress only the very tips until the pleasure was so
total she could not stand it any longer. She cried out,
buckled, fell against him, and in time recovered.

'With soapy hands, Erin began some massaging
of her own. She loved his muscular hardness, loved
the vertical line of body hair which ran from his
chest across his belly and down. She traced its path,
first with a fingertip and then with her tongue,
laughing as Jago begged, 'Further, further, further!'
He raised her to kiss her lips, and for a long time
they stayed pressed together as the water thrummed
down.

How they reached the bed, and more or less dry, Erin did not know, but there they were, tangled and kissing on white sheets. Jago clasped one breast, rounding it with his hand, pointing the peak skywards, the better to cover it with his mouth. She cried out, she whimpered, thrusting herself up. The flames burned, she exalted in their burn. Jago's hand slid to her inner thigh, and again she cried out.

'Erin!' he exclaimed, through clenched teeth. 'Erin, I love you.'

'And I love you,' she vowed.

Holding her hips firm, he entered her, shuddering. Hot as in H O T. But where her heat ended and Jago's began, she did not know. He loved her and she loved him. They were one, moving together.

Oh, the bliss, the agony, the splendour! Thrashing beneath him, Erin offered up all the love she had to give. His love joined hers, mingled, exploded, and together they reached fulfilment.

Afterwards they slept, to make love again later. Held safe in the circle of his arms, Erin nestled closer. Maybe she should cancel her flight home tomorrow? she wondered drowsily. Maybe she should move into the sprawling white house? Maybe she should . . .

'Honey, I must go.'

'No,' she murmured.

'I must. It's nearly——' Presumably he told her the time. 'And I——' Presumably he gave her reasons. Whatever they were, she was too drugged to hear. Sun and love had taken their toll. Jago's voice sounded from a distance. 'Come back when you're ready. If you get in touch with Burt he can pass a message to me wherever I am.' She felt his lips brush her cheek. 'Understand, Erin?'

'Mmm,' she murmured, and fell fast asleep.

CHAPTER NINE

THE removal men gave a blast on their horn in farewell. Erin waved until the van disappeared around a bend in the lane, then walked back indoors. Earlier that day, when curtains had framed the latticed windows, when furniture had been spread throughout the rooms, when the horse brasses pinned to the oak beams had glinted in the sunlight, her home had been cosy. Now, stripped of everything bar the carpets, the cottage felt as barren as a barn.

'Well, that's it. The end of an era,' she said jauntily, joining her mother in the kitchen.

Mrs Page paused in her final wipe round. 'Are you sure you've done the right thing?, she fretted.

'If I haven't, it's too late. There's no turning back, not with my goods and chattels on their way into store, and the new owners moving in here on Monday.'

'But selling up is such a drastic step, Erin. Everything's happened so quickly that I just wonder if you've not rushed in. And why Scotland? Why must you go so far?'

'Scotland isn't Siberia,' she protested. 'You and Dad can always jump in the car and come to see me.'

'Scotland must be five hundred miles away.'

'Four, and in any case I'm only going for six months.'

'Yes, six months in Scotland and then where?' Mrs Page clicked an exasperated tongue. 'Given your present mood it wouldn't surprise me if you *did* disappear to Siberia. Abandoning your writing when you were so nicely established, so nicely settled, makes no sense at all.'

Erin sighed. They had been through this before, several times. 'I wasn't settled, I was in a rut. Now I'm climbing out. Writing's a very solitary occupation and I've been solitary for far too long. I need to meet people.'

'You call showing tourists through a castle meeting people? You could have met people round here.'

'I know everybody round here,' she said patiently, then grinned. 'Cheer up. Maybe a rugged Scots laird will sweep me off my feet and before you know it you'll be knee deep in those grandchildren you're always hankering after.'

Mrs Page gave the tiled worktops a severe double-check, then stashed the cloth away in her shopping basket. 'Kevin asked after you yesterday,' she said, patting her grey hair into tidiness and slipping on her coat. 'Every time I see him, he asks. He's such a nice boy. You could go a long way and not find anyone as nice as Kevin.'

'As far as Scotland? But I've known Kevin since he sat behind me at junior school and pulled my pigtails, and never once felt—drawn. The chances of me walking past his butcher's shop one morning and shouting "Eureka" when I see him weighing out a pound of liver have to be remote.'

'But Kevin would be so—convenient.'

'Like Peter was convenient?'

Mrs Page drew herself up. Although she could not put her finger on it, she sensed criticism. 'We knew Peter's background, we knew he was solid and reliable. We knew his parents because they lived locally, we knew——'

'I thought you were in a hurry to go home and start preparing the dinner while I finish off here?' Erin interrupted. She kissed her mother on the cheek. 'Thanks for all your help. I could never have managed without you.'

Diverted, Mrs Page beamed. 'My pleasure, pet. Yes, I will pop off. We'll be having chicken in lemon sauce with courgettes, one of your favourites. It's lovely to think you'll be living with your father and me again, even if it is just for a few days before you head up to Scotland.' Walking into the hall, she paused. 'Isn't the gas man supposed to be coming to read the meter?'

'Yes, he is. I wonder where he's got to?' Erin checked her watch. 'If he doesn't come soon, he can go and whistle.'

When her mother departed, she plugged in the vacuum. She wanted to leave everything spotless, and all that was needed now was a final tour round with the cleaner. She set to work, tackling one room after another. Even though the cottage did feel like a barn, in reality the dimensions were small and with no furniture to hinder her progress, the task was quickly accomplished. A quarter of an hour later, the carpets were pristine and the cleaner was stacked up by the front door. Still the gas man had not arrived. Where was he? Erin wandered upstairs to perch on the window-seat in the front bedroom. From here she could keep watch.

She drew her bejeaned knees up to her chin, wrapped her arms around her legs, and sighed. Her mother's worries had been fielded off with a perky confidence, but that confidence had an annoying tendency to flow and ebb. It was ebbing now. She suddenly felt timid. Yanking up thirty years' worth of roots demanded strength and resolve, and she wondered whether she had much of both, either, any? A job had been found and the cottage sold at such speed, she had had little time to dwell on the pluses and minuses, but now she began to do her sums.

She was swapping security for insecurity, the known for the unknown, proven success for ... what? Erin bowed her head. Stop evading the issue, she scolded herself. None of this matters. What really matters is why Scotland, why not Florida? Why wasn't she following where her heart led and throwing in her lot with that blond Viking who, two months ago, had said, 'Come back when you're ready. Understand?' She did understand—now. Initially she had floated home with her head full of daydreams; about her and Jago on their wedding day, going off on honeymoon, crooning over their first baby, raising a family together. Together meant man and wife. But as one week, two, three, had passed without any contact between them, so those mind pictures had altered like shapes in a kaleidoscope. The ingredients had remained constant, but . . .

She knew Jago would be leaving her alone on purpose, giving her peace in which to finish the profile, allowing her time to think through what she wanted from life, and she was grateful. Yet didn't this wide berth indicate an inherently casual approach? She did not regard him as nonconformist or unorthodox, like his parents, but he was not a person hidebound by conventionality. The more she thought about things, the more convinced Erin became that although for her the natural progression in their relationship would be marriage, it was not so for Jago. That did not mean that if she went to him he would not love her, would not commit himself to her. She believed he would, but not as a husband. Husband and wife became man and woman.

Man and woman wasn't enough. In her world love and marriage were inextricably intertwined. Love without marriage was a halfway arrangement and she was not a halfway person. Short-term maybe she could accept what her mother would denounce as 'living in sin', long-term—no. The daydreams which had suspended her in mid-air vanished, she had fallen to eerth with a bump. Facts had to be faced. In the show business sphere living together raised no eyebrows, and Jago inhabited that sphere. At thirty-six he was still a bachelor. But the crux of the matter was that he had loved Olivia, lived with her for three years, and yet had not felt the urge to legalise their affair. There had not been a whisper in that direction, either in the cuttings she had read or from Susie. Erin felt empty inside. Few parallels existed between her and Olivia, yet so what? The writing on the wall was clear—Jago was not the marrying kind.

There was a movement in the corner of her eye, and she looked up to glimpse a figure disappearing below the front porch. The gas man, she decided, and ran downstairs.

'Where have you been? I thought you were never coming,' she said in jokey protest, opening the door.

'Hey, those are my lines,' chided a familiar American drawl. Her visitor removed his cap, folded a pair of sunglasses and slipped them into the top pocket of a dark blue leather jacket. 'Have you missed me?' he grinned, as she stood and gaped. 'Never given me a passing thought, eh?'

'Yes, yes, I have.' Her face might be as vacant as a potato, but inside her mind was jigging. She had planned to write on reaching Scotland and explain why their future was doomed, but his arrival had smashed this approach to smithereens. Now Erin wondered how she was supposed to tell him face to face—coolly and calmly—that she wanted what he wasn't prepared to give . . . a wedding ring? Cool and calm was impossible. Jago's proximity had already sent her heart banging inside her breast, made her legs feel shaky. Strange that when common sense demanded she push him away, instinct told her to devour him whole. Discovering her palms were damp, Erin wiped them on the seat of her jeans. 'Would—would you like to come in?' she enquired, backing into the hall.

In reply he slung his suitcase inside, and before she could protest had reached for her.

'Honey, honey,' he murmured, burying his face in the dark clouds of her hair. 'You sure as hell take your time. Okay, I said to come back when you were ready, but to let two months pass without even a hint of when I can expect you—Erin! It seems like two years.'

'Does it?' Her voice was faint. She wished she had backed away further. She wished he would let her go. Also she wished he would hold her close like this for ever.

'Like two centuries. How I've managed to stay away this far is a miracle of self-control.'

His eyes wandered down to her mouth, and she knew he was about to kiss her. Erin pushed back.

'When did you arrive in England?'

'Three hours ago. I took a taxi straight from the airport,' he muttered, his eyes still on her mouth.

'Why didn't you let me know you were coming?'

He sighed, raising his gaze. 'If I had, would you have baked me a cake?' he asked drily. 'Look, toots, it was only last night that my patience finally snapped and I realised no way could I live through another day of you being on one side of the Atlantic and me on the other. I fixed myself a ticket and decided to surprise you.' Ready to enfold her in his arms once more, Jago suddenly noticed the hall's Spartan appearance. 'You've sold up? You're moving out?' he hazarded, and at her nod, hugged her tight, murmuring his delight. 'Erin, you fiend.

Now I understand. Before you joined me you wanted to tie up all the loose ends. I should've known Organised Annie would do the right things in the right order.' He looked around. 'Where's that cat of yours? Has it been sold too, or is it coming with you to the States?'

'The cat's staying with my mother, but——' A deep breath was required. A deep breath was taken. 'I'm not coming to the States.'

'I beg your pardon?'

'I'm not coming. I was going to write and explain. Jago, I just—I don't think we're ... compatible.'

His arms dropped from her. He looked as stunned as if she had punched him in the solar plexus.

'How d' you work that one out?' he demanded. 'I love you and I understood you love me?'

'I do,' she said feebly.

'Well then? On an emotional level we click and physically we have everything going for us. What more do you want?'

Erin felt her colour rising. The 'more' was marriage, but a complex of reasons—pride, the fear of sounding like an accuser, a puritan—tied her tongue.

'We—we come from different countries,' was what she eventually mumbled.

'Agreed.'

'You grew up moving around. I grew up in one place.'

'Agreed.'

'And—er.' The look on his face told her she was not making much headway. 'My background was kind of narrow, and yours was—wide.'

'Agreed. Go on.'

Where could she go? Only to the truth. 'Jago, you and Olivia were together for three years,' she stated, setting off at a cracking pace. 'The two of you were close. You appear to have been together night and day. You cared as much for her career as you did for your own. There was this depth of feeling between you, and yet . . .' The cracking pace met a bump in the road. 'I accept that for some people marriage is a meaningless formality, and don't think I'm criticising because I'm not, but for me—oh Jago,' she wailed, 'you loved Olivia and yet despite that——'

'I didn't love her,' he cut in.

'You—you didn't?' That hadn't been a bump in the road, it had been a hole. Erin felt as if she had fallen into it. 'But Susie told me how——'

'Susie doesn't know the half of it. Nobody does. Do you mind if we sit down?' he enquired. 'I guess I need to explain about Olivia, so we could be talking for quite a while. I'd prefer to do it in comfort.'

'I'm afraid there isn't any comfort, just the stairs or a window-seat.'

'Window-seat,' Jago decided, and gestured for her to lead the way. In the bedroom he plunked himself down opposite her, his back against the oak window surround, his long legs spread with his feet planted firmly on the shaggy white carpet. 'Olivia possessed what I can only describe as a fey quality,' he began. 'She was inconsistent, erratic, and for some inexplicable reason that intrigued me. I knew she was riddled with insecurities, the danger signs

were there very early on, and yet . . .' He looked out
on to the lane where the green-leaved branches of
the sycamores moved in the breeze. 'Like you were
attracted to Edward Lanham for no good reason, so
I was attracted to her. At first things were fine, then
she began to be jealous of my success. There was
nothing I could do. I was what I was. I couldn't
change the past. In time her animosity developed
until it began to poison our lives together.'

'Why didn't you end the relationship?'

'Everyone wondered that. The general opinion
was I was crazy to put up with her.' Jago gave a dry
laugh. 'What they didn't know was that I didn't
have any choice. After a while I got a little sick of
her attitude, and a lot sick of being used, so I said
that I felt we should go our separate ways,' he
explained. 'I wasn't hostile, I just said it didn't make
sense to be causing each other pain. But Olivia
wasn't having any. She started to play the Tragedy
Queen.' He let out a breath. 'If she could act one
tenth as well on stage as she does in real life, she'd
have a shelf full of Oscars. But she can't, that's the
pity of it. However, I was given the full works—the
tears, the pleas, the pathetic pose on the sofa. She
vowed I was the only man she'd ever been able to
trust, that she depended on me in total, and——' He
ran a hand through his hair. 'And when it was all
over I discovered I'd caved in. I allowed us to
hobble on. Mind you, it was hobbling. And it wasn't
long before I decided I really must make the break.
The tears were joined by heavier artillery the second
time around. Olivia made a few choice statements
like, "If you feel this way I'd be better off under a

bus" and "If you send me away, my life might as well end".'

Erin felt gooseflesh cover her arms. 'She was threatening suicide?' she asked in horror.

He nodded, his face grim. 'But it didn't stop at threatening. For a long time after that, even though I rebelled against what was emotional blackmail, I handled her with kid gloves. Then one day, it got too much. I blew my top. I said everything I'd said before, how living together was no good for either of us, in fact it was hell on earth, and that if she wasn't prepared to move out of my apartment, I was! Much to my surprise, she promised she'd be gone the next day. That night I arrived back late from the theatre and the moment I unlocked the door I could sense something was wrong. There was a silence, an eerie silence.' Jago rubbed the back of his neck. 'God, I go hot and cold now, just thinking about it. I knew Olivia had to be there and I called out. No answer. I charged around and found her in the bedroom with pill bottles strewn around, all empty. I hauled her into the bathroom, stuck my fingers down her throat and made her sick. She began to revive. When the doctor arrived I think I needed him more than she did! He took me to one side and dismissed what she'd done as attention seeking. He said she'd taken nowhere near enough pills to finish herself off, that it had just been a gesture. Some gesture! But after that I guess I became paranoid. It seemed like if I said one wrong word Olivia might throw herself off a high tower.'

'Did she try anything again?' Erin asked, in a hushed tone.

'She didn't need to. I wasn't having her ending her life because of me. We continued to hobble on, with me giving up daily prayers that either she'd strike lucky in her career or would switch herself to some other guy.'

'And then the crash intervened?'

'Yeah.' Jago turned from the window and slumped forward, clasping his hands between his knees. For a moment he was thoughtful. 'Susie and I had planned to visit Thailand together; she wanted to see the temples Ursula had raved over, I wanted to visit my birthplace. Everything was fixed, then Olivia muscled in. My sister was not pleased.'

'I can imagine!'

He gave a wry smile. 'I did my best to persuade Olivia the vacation was a family jaunt, but she went into the old sob routine, made a few oblique threats, and to cut a long story short, she came with us to Thailand. One day we hired a car and decided to visit a village where there was a market and a cultural show. At first I drove, but I'd picked up a bug, one of those twenty-four hour things, and I began to feel lousy. It ended up with Olivia driving, Susie reading the map, and me lying flat out in the back. Susie's a pathetic navigator and we took a wrong turn. She and Olivia started to bicker, I sat up, and the next thing I knew there was this pick-up truck roaring straight at us on the wrong side of the road. I crawled out of the wreckage and amazingly I was fine, cut and bruised, but that was all. Olivia was also unhurt. But Susie——' He took a snatched breath. 'She was lying there, so still. It was obvious she'd been seriously injured, but how could I get help? The next few hours were the worst in my life. The guys in the pick-up were labourers, they didn't speak any English and, given the chance, I think they'd have just scooted off. But I started to rant and rave, and I managed to get them to take me to the nearest village. It seemed to be a hundred miles away. By the time we arrived I was frantic. Nobody there spoke English either, but somehow it filtered through that an ambulance should be summoned. A shopkeeper telephoned, then had someone drive me back to the car. Olivia'd been looking after Susie, and when I arrived she promptly laid into me for leaving her alone there for so long!' He wiped a hand across his brow. 'All I could do was pin my hopes on that ambulance materialising, but it took hours to arrive and in all that time Susie never moved. I thought she was going to die. She nearly did.' Jago's face crumpled. 'Maybe if I'd been able to get help to her sooner she wouldn't be stuck in a wheelchair now,' he muttered.

Erin laid her hand on his arm. 'You don't know that,' she said gently.

'No.' When he looked at her, his eyes were wet.

'And Susie stayed in hospital in Thailand for several months?' she prompted.

He gave a noisy sniff and nodded. 'I was warned her bones might take a long time to settle. I was also warned her medical care wouldn't come cheap. Maybe they were fleecing me, I don't know, but I wasn't in any position to argue. I'd been geared up to start rehearsals for a Broadway play the following week, so I got in touch and said my return had been delayed. The response was an ultimatum, be there in a fortnight or else!'

'You really were being hanged, drawn and quartered,' she sympathised.

'With a vengeance. I needed to be in that play because it was imperative I earn money. I rang round my brothers and sisters and somehow we managed to work out a way of having someone in Bangkok with Susie for the foreseeable future. The only problem was a gap between me returning to the States and one of my sisters arriving to take over. As it was just a few days, I asked Olivia if she'd fill in.' Jago balled his fists. 'But that damn woman——'

'She wouldn't?

He shook his head. 'I accept she'd had a shock, I accept she may have had some sort of guilt hang-up, but even so. My God, that accident concentrated her mind wonderfully. She said she couldn't stay, that I couldn't expect her to stay because she wasn't family, was she? In fact, she'd known for a long time she didn't mean much to me and I most certainly did not mean much to her. I had been right, we would be much better off apart. Zoom— her bags were packed and she was boarding a plane. I stayed with Susie until my other sister arrived, then set off home.'

'To be out of work?'

'No I managed to cling on to my part in the play by the skin of my teeth.'

'So it was exit Olivia, stage left?'

'Yeah. She'd gone by the time I arrived back at my apartment. I've never heard from her since.' Jago frowned. 'She's the real reason why I stopped you writing about Susie in your profile. You see, I don't know how she'd react. If the facts were publicised and a reporter knocked on her door asking questions about how she'd been driving at the time my sister had been crippled, what would she do? Maybe she wouldn't give a damn, but maybe Olivia would go the other way, get depressed, take pills? It's enough that Susie is like she is without another life being damaged.'

'Which is why you kept the accident out of the papers?' Erin surmised.

'It wasn't difficult. Thailand isn't gossip column country.' Jago cast her a glance. 'I know I should have told you all this before, but——'

'But you don't find sharing things easy?'

He grinned. 'Isn't that becoming a fallacy? I seem to be sharing one hell of a lot with you.' He paused, his blue eyes intent. 'Isn't it time you shared something with me?'

'Like what?'

'Like the real reason for this——' he thought better, and substituted a less impolite word for the one he had been ready to use '— tosh about you not coming to the States.'

'Oh.'

'Yes, oh.' There was the hint of a smile. 'If it's any help, I have somehow gained the impression you believe I'm anti-marriage?'

Erin felt skewered. 'Aren't you? You—you have reached the grand old age of thirty-six without tying any knots,' she protested. 'And Olivia apart, there have been other relationships, and——' Saying exactly what she wanted to say remained a stumbling block.

Jago helped again. 'And I've never made them permanent? Want to know why? Maybe this is a paradox, but it's out of respect for the institution of marriage that I've preferred to co-habit. I happen to believe marriage is for ever, and finding someone I wanted to live with for ever was a problem. However, a while back this lady author in beautifully short shorts woke me up one morning, and in no time at all was throwing herself on top of me and squirming around in a most unladylike fashion. Now I knew from the start we weren't compatible. After all, she's easy with seven-letter words, while I use four. She's a straight-A type, while I'm lucky if I scrape by with Cs. She says "autumn" while I say "fall" but——' He reached for her hand, mingling his fingers with hers. 'Will you marry me?'

He had unlocked the door to paradise and led her inside.

'Yes, yes, *yes*!'

Even if it had been two months since they had kissed, his mouth was just as she remembered—warm, moist and eager. The effect it had was just as she remembered, too. Her blood chased, her heart thumped against his. There came that bitter-sweet hunger, that spiralling, an ache.

'I love you, I love you, I love you.'

The words moved between them, meshing with sighs, kisses, hugs.

'I was supposed to be going to Scotland,' Erin remembered, after a long time.

'Scotland?' He sounded as disgusted as her

mother. 'Are you researching a Scots Edwardian?'

'No. I've found a post as a tourist guide. You see, after I left Florida——'

'And me.'

'Yes, after I left you.' She kissed his cheek. 'After I left I started thinking. I realised the best way to break the stranglehold my writing had was to give it up for a while, take a sabbatical. I completed your profile, handed the book over to Cleo, and the very next day I happened to see an advertisement for a tourist guide.'

'You never told Cleo you wanted a sabbatical,' Jago intruded.

'Not then. I phoned her last night. I wanted to have everything cut and dried, just in case she protested.'

'Did she?'

Erin laughed wryly. 'No. She said to hell with her ten per cent, she was just happy I'd got my priorities right at last, though she did think Scotland an odd direction to head for.'

'It should've been the States?' Jago suggested.

'As she noticeably inserted a long screed about how she could tell from the profile that I thought you were a wonderful man—yes, that was the general impression.'

'Do you think I'm wonderful?'

Grinning, she folded her arms and weighed him up.

'Hmm, your nose is a bit skew-whiff.'

He made a grab for her. 'I said wonderful, not perfect. Besides, if I stand sideways you can't tell my nose's off-centre. Not that I intend to spend the rest of my life standing sideways-on to you. There are other positions which interest me more. Like me lying on top of you, or you lying on top of me, or——'

'Jago!' she protested, and laughingly succumbed to a second batch of kisses. 'How did you know I hadn't warned Cleo I'd be taking a sabbatical?' Erin queried, surfacing.

'Because I kept track of you through her. How was I supposed to carry on for two months without a single word?' he appealed.

'She never said you'd been in touch.'

'I asked her to keep quiet. The ball was in your court,' he pointed out, 'and I didn't want to crowd you.'

'You didn't!'

'From now on I will,' he promised.

'How can I make a graceful exit from the job in Scotland?' she wondered vaguely, as Jago began to kiss her again.

'Search me.'

'And how do I break it to my mother that her grandchildren will be wearing baseball caps?'

'Search me.'

Erin slid off the window-seat and into his waiting arms. The shaggy white carpet felt far more erotic than any water-bed.

'And what do I do if the gas man comes to read the meter in the next half hour?'

'Search me. You would like to, wouldn't you?' he murmured, his mouth finding hers.

'Mmm.' She started by unbuttoning his shirt.

'I was supposed to tell you I've landed a role in a

film,' he said, helping her and thus speeding up the process. He also shucked off his leather jacket. 'And I was also supposed to say that your solution to the Susie problem worked like a dream. She and Robert have a house. It's being renovated right now, but will be ready in a couple of months when they're due to be married. After us. I was also supposed to tell you I've made enquiries and we can get a special licence. Also—oh hell,' he sighed, pressing her back on to the carpet. 'When am I ever going to find time to say all these things?'

'Search me,' Erin smiled.

Jago did.

Coming Next Month

Available in April wherever paperback books are sold, or through
Harlequin Reader Service:

In the U.S.
P.O. Box 1397
Buffalo, N.Y.
14240-1397

In Canada
P.O. Box 603
Fort Erie, Ontario
L2A 5X3

PATRICIA MATTHEWS

America's First Lady of Romance upholds her long standing reputation as a bestselling romance novelist with . . .

Enchanted

Caught in the steamy heat of America's New South, Rebecca Trenton finds herself torn between two brothers—she yearns for one but a dark secret binds her to the other.

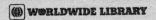

Can you keep a secret?

You can keep this one plus 4 free novels